HARLEQUIN

INTRIGUE

WYOMING COWBOY SNIPER

NICOLE HELM

HARLEQUIN

INTRIGUE

Edge-of-your-seat intrigue, fearless romance

AVAILABLE THIS MONTH

#1851 SHOW OF FORCE
Declan's Defenders
Elle James

#1852 SMOKIES SPECIAL AGENT
The Mighty McKenzies
Lena Diaz

#1853 SNOWBOUND SUSPICION
Eagle Mountain Murder Mystery: Winter Storm Wedding
Cindi Myers

#1854 WYOMING COWBOY SNIPER
Carsons & Delaneys: Battle Tested
Nicole Helm

#1855 CRIMINAL BEHAVIOR
Twilight's Children
Amanda Stevens

#1856 K-9 DEFENSE
Elizabeth Heiter

ISBN-13: 978-1-335-64084-0

EAN

From passionate, suspenseful and dramatic love stories to inspirational or historical, Harlequin offers different lines to satisfy every romance reader.

New books available every month.

HILPATMIFC0519

She was a Carson. He was a Delaney. They'd never understand each other.

But damn, Dylan wanted to. Understand her. Have her understand him. He wanted to chase this power that arced between them. But it wasn't the time or place. "Right now we'll focus on getting out of here."

When the tension crept into her shoulders, he squeezed. "Don't worry. I'll protect you. I'm an expert."

She didn't laugh or even crack a smile, but the moment held. And in that moment he needed her to believe that he'd protect her with everything he was.

He placed his own hand over her stomach. "I'll protect you both."

She took a sharp breath in, then slowly let it out. Then her hand reached out and cupped his jaw. His chest clutched, a metal fist squeezing against his heart, and then his lungs.

Her dark eyes were rich and deep and fathomless. He saw something he'd never seen in her before. Warmth. Care.

You're losing it, Delaney.

"Protect all three of us," Vanessa whispered, and then pressed her mouth to his.

WYOMING COWBOY SNIPER

NICOLE HELM

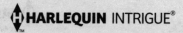

HARLEQUIN INTRIGUE®

For opposites who attract.

ISBN-13: 978-1-335-64084-0

Wyoming Cowboy Sniper

Copyright © 2019 by Nicole Helm

Recycling programs
for this product may
not exist in your area.

Printed in U.S.A.

www.Harlequin.com

Nicole Helm grew up with her nose in a book and the dream of one day becoming a writer. Luckily, after a few failed career choices, she gets to follow that dream— writing down-to-earth contemporary romance and romantic suspense. From farmers to cowboys, Midwest to *the* West, Nicole writes stories about people finding themselves and finding love in the process. She lives in Missouri with her husband and two sons and dreams of someday owning a barn.

Books by Nicole Helm

Harlequin Intrigue

Carsons & Delaneys: Battle Tested

Wyoming Cowboy Marine
Wyoming Cowboy Sniper

Carsons & Delaneys

Wyoming Cowboy Justice
Wyoming Cowboy Protection
Wyoming Christmas Ransom

Stone Cold Texas Ranger
Stone Cold Undercover Agent
Stone Cold Christmas Ranger

Harlequin Superromance

A Farmers' Market Story

All I Have
All I Am
All I Want

Falling for the New Guy
Too Friendly to Date
Too Close to Resist

Visit the Author Profile page at Harlequin.com.

CAST OF CHARACTERS

Vanessa Carson—A Carson who takes her bad-girl reputation very seriously. She runs the mechanic shop in town and can't believe she got drunk enough to sleep with Dylan Delaney, especially when she finds out she's pregnant.

Dylan Delaney—A Delaney who takes his good-guy reputation very seriously. He manages the Delaney Bank and can't believe he lost control enough at his sister's wedding to get drunk and end up in Vanessa's bed. But when he and Vanessa are kidnapped by possible bank robbers, Dylan's secret past might just save them both.

Adele Oscar—The only other person working at the bank when the robbery and kidnapping occur. She's kidnapped with Dylan and Vanessa, but something isn't quite right about her.

Laurel Delaney-Carson—Dylan's sister and Vanessa's sister-in-law, Laurel is the detective for the Bent County sheriff's department, and she's determined to figure out what happened to Dylan and Vanessa.

Grady Carson—Laurel's husband and Vanessa's brother.

Deputy Hart—Due to Laurel's pregnancy, Laurel is training Deputy Hart to take her place as detective for the Bent County sheriff's department.

Prologue

Dylan Delaney considered the scene around him an atrocity: Carsons and Delaneys of Bent, Wyoming, not just mingling in the same yard but celebrating.

Celebrating the marriage of his sister—an upstanding, rule-following sheriff's deputy with too good of a heart—to a no-good, lying, cheating, *saloon-owning* Carson.

The fact his sister looked so happy as she danced with her newly pronounced husband was the only reason Dylan was keeping his mouth shut. That and a well-stocked makeshift bar in the Carson barn that had been transformed into a wedding venue for Laurel and Grady.

Dylan had been bred to hate Carsons and what they represented his whole life. Delaneys were better than thieving, low-class, lying Carsons— and had been since the town had been founded back in the eighteen hundreds.

Dylan's siblings had always been too soft.

Though Jen had held strong with him, Cam and Laurel were growing even softer in adulthood as they mixed themselves up with Carsons.

Romantically of all things.

Dylan had prided himself on being hard. On being *better*. Half his siblings had been happy to ignore the calling of the Delaney name, but he'd used everything he had in him to live up to it.

If it felt hollow in the face of his sister happily marrying Grady Carson, he'd ignore it.

"Worried about your precious bloodline, Delaney?"

Dylan sneered. Normally, he wouldn't. Normally, he'd be cool, collected and cuttingly disdainful of Vanessa Carson even breathing the same air as him, let alone addressing him. But the liquor was smoothing out just enough of his senses for him to forget he never engaged with the Carson he hated the most.

"Aren't you worried about catching a little law and order? Ruining that bad-girl reputation of yours?" Dylan smiled, the way he would have smiled at a dirty child who'd just smeared mud over his freshly dry-cleaned suit.

She wore the same shade of black as his suit, but not in a sedate cocktail dress that might have befit a wedding. He'd have even given a pass to a funeralesque sundress, because it was a rather casual affair all in all, and it felt like a funeral on his end.

But no. Vanessa wore tight leather pants and some kind of contraption on top that flowed behind her like a cape down to her knees. It knotted in the front above her belly button. A little gold hoop dangled there, mocking him.

He was so attracted to her, it hurt. He hated himself for that purely animalistic reaction that he'd always, *always* refused to act on. He'd dealt with cosmic jokes his whole life. This was just another one to be put away and ignored. He was stronger than the cosmos. Had to be.

She flashed a grin meant to peel the skin off his face. "My bad-girl reputation is rock-hard solid, babe." She sauntered around Dylan and the makeshift bar, then started looking through the collection of bottles and cans.

The hired bartender blinked at her, clearly caught off guard and having no idea what to do despite making a living from serving drunk and rowdy wedding guests. "I can get you what you—"

"No worries." She nudged the bartender away and rummaged around, then poured herself an impressive and possibly lethal combination of alcohol. She lifted her cup in Dylan's direction, which was when he realized he'd been watching her. She drank deeply.

"If that was for my benefit, color me unimpressed," he muttered, looking away from that long slender neck and the way long wisps of midnight-black hair danced around her face.

"Baby, I wouldn't do anything for your benefit, even if you were on fire," Vanessa said, her voice a smooth purr.

He refused to let his body react. "Someone's going to be carrying you out of here if you drink all that."

She laughed, low and smoky. It slithered through him like—

Like nothing.

"I could shoot you under the table, sweetheart."

"Wanna bet?" he muttered, forcing himself to stare ahead even though he could feel her come to stand next to him.

She laughed again, the sound so arousing he wanted to bash his own head in.

"I know you didn't just say that to me, Delaney. You're not that stupid."

Which poked at all the reactions he kept locked far, far away. Apparently the rather potent drinks he'd been downing in swift succession were the key to unlocking them. "I'll repeat it, then. Want to bet?" He enunciated each word with exaggerated precision as he turned to look at her.

She smirked, somehow a few inches shorter than

him even though she always seemed to take up so much space. "Oh, I'll take that bet. How much?"

He named a sum he knew she couldn't possibly afford.

She rolled her eyes and waved a dismissive hand that glinted silver and gold with an impressive array of rings, including more than one in the shape of a skull or dagger.

He despised her. Every inch of her. Which he drank in against his will.

"Delaneys love to flaunt their money."

He flashed a wolfish grin, enjoying far too much the way her eyes narrowed as if preparing to ward him off. *Good luck, little girl.* "Chicken?"

Some little voice in the back of his head reminded him of propriety. Reminded him of his place in Bent and the fact that getting in a drinking competition with Vanessa would only end in embarrassment and trouble. It went against everything he believed and stood for, and he should just walk away.

He stood where he was and ignored that voice.

When he woke up the next morning, definitely not in his own bed, ignoring that voice was the last thing he remembered.

VANESSA WAS DYING. From the inside out. So, so many bad decisions made last night. But it was her brother's fault for marrying a Delaney. That she was sure of.

She groaned, rolling over in bed as her stomach roiled in protest. She'd had her fair share of hangovers, but this one was truly something.

And now she was hallucinating.

Had to be. Because there was no way on God's green earth that Dylan Delaney was in her bed.

No *Delaney man* was *naked* in her bed, in the middle of her apartment above her mechanic shop. She looked to the left. There was her little kitchen, the hall with the bathroom door. She looked to the right, at the door to the stairs down to the shop, and in that line of vision was clearly a man.

As she blinked at that shape of a man next to her, it was Dylan's dark eyes that widened and sharpened. It was every gorgeous plane of Dylan Delaney's face that went very, very hard.

Vanessa closed her eyes tight, counted to ten in a whisper. It had to be a dream. It had to be an alcohol-induced mirage. It had to be anything but the truth.

But when she was done counting, Dylan was still there.

"Apparently bad dreams do come true," Dylan said, his voice all delicious rough gravel.

Get yourself together. Nothing about Dylan Delaney is delicious.

She watched, horrified, really she was horrified and not intrigued at all, as he flung the covers—*her* covers—off of him and stood, clearly having no compunction about being *naked in her room*.

With jerky movements, he pulled on his pants from last night. Last night. She'd…

"You can't tell anyone." If she'd been feeling better she would have kept that inside. Ignored the panic and held on to the upper hand. But she was *dying*, and she'd apparently slept with Dylan Delaney.

She remembered nothing. Nothing about last night beyond the wedding ceremony where her rough-and-tumble brother had promised himself forever to goody-two-shoes Laurel Delaney. A *cop*.

Beyond that, everything got fuzzier and fuzzier until…

Best kiss of your life.

Ha! She'd been drunk. How would she have known?

Dylan gave her one smoldering look—enough her heart started pumping overtime and her whole body seemed to blaze with heat. She could almost, *almost* picture them together, feel his big rough hands on her—

But Dylan Delaney, a bank manager, did not have rough hands. She was hallucinating. And was that a *tattoo* on his chest that disappeared as he pulled his shirt on and began to button it?

"Who on *earth* do you think I'd tell about this horrifying lapse in judgment?" he said disgustedly.

It didn't sting, because she felt the same way. Except *lapse in judgment* was way too tame. *Catastrophe of epic proportions* was more appropriate.

A catastrophe she would also blame on Grady, because if he hadn't married a Delaney, she wouldn't have gotten drunk enough to *sleep* with one.

Dylan was now completely dressed, and she was still naked in her bed. *Naked.*

"We'll both forget this ever happened," Dylan said. No. He demanded it, like she was a peon to be ordered about. But even she couldn't work up contrariness at his tone when *this* had happened.

"I don't even know *what* happened. We didn't really…" But he'd been naked, and she was naked so…

"I don't remember either. So we'll just say we didn't."

"But—"

"We didn't," he said firmly, patting down his pockets. "I have my wallet. No keys."

"Surely neither of us were stupid enough to drive."

"Surely neither of us were stupid enough to

have someone drive us *together* anywhere." He sighed, running an agitated hand through sleep-tousled hair. He did not look like his normal slick self. He was disheveled and...

Appealing.

No, not that.

"Hate sex is a thing," she blurted, feeling un-accountably out of control and nervous. Which did not make any sense, but she couldn't seem to straighten herself out. It had to be the hangover and all the booze still in her system.

He scowled, and Vanessa didn't understand why her eyes wanted to track the small lines around his mouth or note the way dark stubble dotted his chin where it had been smooth last night.

There was something compelling about him. She'd admit it now and regain some of her control. They were polar opposites, and sometimes when polar opposites got drunk enough, they ended up attracting.

She'd swear off alcohol for the rest of her life right here, right now.

"Hate sex is not a *thing*. Not for me it's not."

"Apparently for drunk you it was."

He pinched the bridge of his nose. "I'm leaving. We'll never speak of this again. And if anyone saw us..."

"We lie," Vanessa supplied for him.

He seemed startled by that word, but what else was there to do?

Eventually, he gave a sharp nod. "Through our teeth." He turned and strode out her apartment door.

Vanessa stared at the ceiling, hoping she never, ever remembered what had transpired and willing herself to forget about it for good.

Chapter One

Vanessa Carson was not a coward. In her entire life, she'd never backed down from an insult, a challenge or a fist. She'd faced all three of those things practically since she'd been born, and yet none of it held a candle to this moment.

She sat in the driver's seat of her ancient sedan in the back parking lot of Delaney Bank. She preferred her motorcycle but… Without thinking the movement through, she placed her hand over her stomach. It was starting to round, just a little bit. No one else would notice, but she could tell. It wouldn't be long before other people would be able to tell, as well.

The morning sickness had been hell, but it seemed to dissipate more every day. She'd taken to eating better, and she'd sworn off alcohol for different reasons ever since that night. Her doctor said she and baby were healthy as a horse.

Luckily, she was surrounded by clueless men for the most part, so no one in her life had any idea. She was convinced it was paranoia that on more than one occasion she'd caught her cousin-in-law or new sister-in-law staring at her with a considering gaze when she did something like eat a veggie plate or pass on another hit of caffeine.

Paranoia or not, she had to face the music before anyone actually put the puzzle together. Had to. Before the music told him itself.

You are not a coward.

She repeated those words with every step toward the bank. She had never once stepped foot in Delaney Bank, would have rather chewed her own arm off—or simply driven the twenty-plus minutes to Fremont whenever she needed a bank.

But this wasn't about asking for a loan or sullying the white halls of such an upstanding establishment run by the Delaneys. It was about the very unfortunate truth.

She was going to have Dylan Delaney's baby.

For a few weeks she'd considered running away. Disappearing. Grady would likely try to find her, with her cousins Noah and Ty not far behind him. But it would have been possible if she'd played her cards right. Eventually, they'd have given up on her. Maybe.

But Bent was her home. Her life. Her mechanic shop was everything she'd built her life on. She'd paid in blood, sweat and tears for it. She wasn't ever going to let a Delaney scare her into running away.

Your baby is half Delaney.

She paused at the corner of the bank building. Ruthlessly, she reminded herself Dylan wouldn't want anyone to know that any more than she did. He'd agree to her plan. He had to. He'd *never* risk his reputation just to be a part of his baby's life.

Which was why she had to tell him. He'd be spiteful if he found out some other way. She needed this to be quick, easy and painless. Which meant she couldn't just stand here.

She heard a noise from behind her and turned to see a back door opening. Dylan stepped out, looking perfectly dapper in a suit with a briefcase clutched in his hand. He slid sunglasses onto his face in defense of the setting sun, his dark looks tinged with gold in the fading light.

She'd never understood her reaction to him—a tug, a *want*. No matter how much she knew she did not want the uptight, soft banker boy, something deep inside of her begged to differ.

Luckily, she was a smart woman who knew when not to listen to stupid feelings. She just needed to explain to him how things were going to be, and be done with him for good.

"Dylan."

He startled, as if he recognized her voice instantly and how incongruous it was at his precious bank. He immediately scanned the lot before turning his gaze to her.

When he'd seen there was no one else around he took a few steps toward her, suspicious and uncomfortable, but not sneery. She would have preferred a little sneery to get her back up.

"Vanessa," he said, his voice cool and clipped, though not nasty.

"Dylan. We need to talk."

He raised an eyebrow. Such a disdainful look, and yet she didn't feel that same animosity from him she'd always had when they'd been growing up. They'd avoided each other even more carefully than usual since Laurel and Grady's wedding, which was hard to do in a small town when your siblings were married. But they'd done it.

Still, there'd been a cooling of antagonism on both their parts. Perhaps they now knew a little too well where unchecked dislike could lead. Being apathetic worked a heck of a lot better.

But she wished he'd be nasty, so she could be angry and defensive instead of so nervous she felt sick.

This is better. You can be calm and collected and show him he's not the only one with some control.

"We really need to talk," Vanessa repeated when he said nothing. "Privately."

Again he scanned the lot and seemed satisfied no one lurked in the dusky shadows. "Follow me."

He used a key card on a pad outside the door he'd come out of, then pulled it open and gestured her inside. She went, chin too high and sharp, shoulders back and braced for a fight.

But it wouldn't be a fight. It would be a quick, informative conversation, and then she'd walk right out of the bank with this awful weight off her shoulders. She wouldn't run her mouth. She'd just say it plain.

He stepped inside, the door closing behind him with a definitive slap. With a nod, he moved down the hallway, leading her to another door—this one glass. Inside was a fancy office. Evidently his, since his name was printed on the glass.

"You know, in my shop I don't have to put my own name on the door to my office."

"I'm guessing, in your shop, you're not entertaining wealthy clients in your office."

She flashed him a hard-edged grin. "You'd be surprised who likes me doing the oil change on their car."

His lips pressed together. She couldn't help but remember him not as the slick, suited businessman who stood before her but as the rumpled, slightly shaken man she'd woken up with that morning all those months ago.

He set his briefcase down and took a seat behind the big, gleaming desk, then ran a hand over the lapel of his suit jacket. He looked impossibly elegant. He wasn't like his siblings. They were the down-home noble type. Laurel the cop, Cam the former marine and Jen the shopkeeper.

Dylan had style—with an edge to it. She didn't know why he stayed in Bent when he was clearly meant to be somewhere a lot more posh than this nowhere Wyoming town.

She didn't know why she had this odd memory of his hands on her feeling *right*.

Just insanity and liquor, she supposed.

"What did you need to discuss?" he asked in the cool, detached voice he'd almost always used on her. Even when they'd been in the same class in first grade, he'd spoken like that to her at the age of seven. Like he was inherently better.

It should have put her back up, but all she could do was stare at him behind his big desk, looking imposing and important in this big, fancy bank office.

She swallowed as an unexpected emotion swamped her. Regret. It was a shame the way her baby had been conceived because this whole Delaney legacy belonged to him or her too.

Money. The kind of reputation people slaved a lifetime to never live up to. The baby wouldn't even have to deal with being the first commingling of Carson and Delaney. Laurel and Grady would always take whatever heat people blamed on a foolish curse, because they'd promised to love each other in front of God himself.

Not everyone in town took the feud between the Carson and Delaney families as seriously as she did, and not everyone in town believed the old tale that if a Carson and Delaney ever fell in love, the town itself would be cursed to destruction.

A story passed down from generation to generation since the Carsons had accused Delaneys of stealing their land back in the eighteen hundreds.

Enough people believed it to make it a *thing*.

The fact Bent hadn't immediately crumbled or been struck by lightning didn't soothe the most superstitious. They were still waiting for it. As for Vanessa, she was more of a take-life-as-it-comes type of girl. She'd deal with a curse if there was one, and she wouldn't be surprised if life went on as it always had.

"I know you're not here for the view. Or a repeat performance," Dylan said, shocking her out of her reverie.

Repeat… She clamped her jaw shut so it wouldn't drop. No one ever turned her off-center like this.

It was the baby softening all her edges. Which was fine and dandy, once she'd done her business. She was determined to be a good mother—the kind hers had never been—where her kid came first and foremost. And not one man was going to ruin that for *her* kid. She'd soften every last edge, sand off her tattoos and cut out her own swearing, drinking, idiot tongue if it meant giving this baby the kind of idyllic childhood she'd never had.

Which meant no strife with the father of the baby, even if Vanessa didn't plan on him being involved.

The best way not to have any strife was to be quick and to the point. She took a deep breath in and let it out, forcing herself to meet Dylan's dark, imposing gaze.

"I'm pregnant."

THE WORDS LANDED like a blow, the kind that had your ears ringing and your eyes seeing stars. Even as Dylan's brain scrambled to make sense of those two simple words, he desperately held on to his composure.

In business, composure was everything.

This wasn't business.

Pregnant. Baby. She was telling him she was pregnant and that meant…

He opened his mouth to speak, though he wasn't sure what it was he meant to say. No words or sound came out, anyway.

"I'm not asking you for anything," she said clearly. Her gaze was calm, direct, but he saw the way she clutched her hands together in her lap. For a woman like Vanessa she might as well have been shaking in her boots. "I'd rather—"

"Yes, I can imagine all you'd rather," he muttered. He glanced at her stomach where her hands were clutched. There was no evidence a child grew there, but one did and it was his.

His.

His heart squeezed as if gripped by some iron outside force, a mix of panic and awe. Mostly panic, he assured himself.

"But if I didn't tell you, you'd figure it out and assume. So I'm telling you. You don't need to worry or do anything. I'll keep your part in this a secret and raise this baby myself." Her hands squeezed harder, and he couldn't seem to bring himself to lift his gaze from them to meet hers.

"Yourself," he repeated stupidly.

"Yes. I'm capable. Maybe I don't look like the most maternal—"

"I'm not challenging you, Vanessa," he snapped, looking away from her hands. Her eyes were storms of a million things. Things he didn't want to consider.

But she was pregnant with his child. *His* child. Hell.

"Regardless," she said, sounding surprisingly prim. "I wanted to be clear that I'll be taking care of everything. As long as you don't yap, we'll be fine."

"Fine," he echoed. Fine. This was not fine.

She began to stand.

"Where the hell do you think you're going?"

She raised her eyebrows. "Home. I told you what I had to say and—"

"And you think I'd just step back and ignore the fact I have a child? You honestly thought you'd make your little announcement and that would be it?"

Her eyes went cool, the nervousness in her clutched hands gone as they came to rest on the arms of the chair. "Obviously, I considered you'd be obnoxious, but I held out hope you'd understand that yes, that's it. Because it's a Carson child."

He stood, pressing his hands to the shiny surface of his desk in an effort to center himself and leash his anger. "Half Delaney."

She folded her arms across her chest and gave him one of those patented Vanessa Carson, *you-are-a-bug-to-be-scraped-off-my-boot* looks. "Are you suggesting we cut the baby in half?" she asked dryly.

"I'm not suggesting anything. You're not giving me time to suggest anything. You've dropped your bomb and now seem to think you're going to waltz out of here and leave me to deal with the fallout."

"I believe that's usually how bombs are dropped," she replied. She was back to herself. Sharp, dismissive and oh so sure she was better than him.

But she hadn't been for a few minutes, and she was carrying his baby. His child.

A living, breathing *human being*.

He sat back down. The weight of it floored him. "I can't… How long? It'd be…" He did the math. "You've been sitting on this for a while."

She shrugged. She wore jeans and a long-sleeved T-shirt. Heavy black boots. Even with her tattoos covered, she looked like trouble. She always had. He didn't know why he'd think pregnancy would change it.

He focused on her. On the gleaming silver skull ring on her thumb. The way her hair seemed all that much blacker against the fair, freckled skin of her cheeks. Sharp edges with surprising hints of vulnerability.

And she was carrying his child.

She sighed heavily. "Look, I don't know what you think sitting there staring at me is going to accomplish, but this is how things are going to be. I have the kid, tell people the father's some random out-of-towner. I live my life and you live yours."

"Knowing your child is mine."

"Consider yourself a sperm donor."

"I will not," he said, managing to keep his voice as even as hers. It was a hard-won thing. "I don't know if you're trying to be difficult or if it just comes naturally, but this is not a *small* thing. It's a huge, bomb-sized thing."

"You seem pretty calm and collected to me," she muttered.

"Years of practice," he said through clenched teeth. The lies he'd told and the things he'd seen. Yes, he'd had *years* of practice in how to appear calm when he was anything but. In control of a world that would not bend to his will—here in Bent or out there where he'd lived his secret life.

Now this. He wanted to be angry, but every time it spurted up, this strange weight settled over him. *Calm* wasn't the right word for it. There was something like a flash of her, from that night. Something he should remember and couldn't. A softness. A rightness.

He shook it away, but he couldn't shake away the realization he didn't have a choice here. She thought he could walk away, turn his back on his own child, and he wouldn't in a million years.

Which meant he had to find common ground with the one person in this whole town—and possibly world—he wasn't sure he could.

There had to be common ground here though, whether he liked it or not. They had to find a compromise.

Something had changed that night, and not just the life it had created. The animosity between him and Vanessa had dulled. Or maybe it was watching Laurel and Grady these past few months. No matter how much grief they got from the town or Dad, they laughed and smiled and…didn't care. Something had changed inside of them so they didn't care.

Dylan had made a child. It was time to not care. "Vanessa."

The distinct sound of a gun being fired jolted them both. It had come from the front. Dylan was on his feet in seconds.

"Stay here," he ordered.

"Stay *here*?" Vanessa repeated incredulously. "You can't… Was that a gun?"

But he was already striding out of his office. He made it not even halfway down the hall before he heard footsteps behind him.

He whirled on Vanessa. "I told you—"

"Was that a gun? We should call someone! Why are you running toward it?"

He didn't have time to explain, but she could call. "Go back to my office, lock the door from the inside and dial 911. Tell them you heard two shots fired in the lobby. One employee inside, not sure about customers. Go."

He nudged her back toward the office.

"Aren't you coming with me?"

"I have to make sure Adele—"

Two masked men slammed through the door from the bank lobby. It was a robbery. Possibly the stupidest of all crimes in this day and age. Surely Adele had hit the alarm and these two men would be caught before they even tried to leave.

Dylan glanced down at the assault rifles they each carried. Unless they'd shot her first. He felt the horror move through him, but quickly pushed it aside. Compartmentalized and assessed the situation.

Two armed robbers in front of him. The Carson woman, pregnant with his baby, behind him.

And he'd thought it was going to be your average Monday.

Chapter Two

Vanessa tried to think, but unfamiliar panic tickled the back of her throat. Masked men with guns. She'd faced a lot of bad crap in her life, but this was a first. Fear had turned her body to lead.

"Office," Dylan said under his breath. He didn't look back at her, just ordered her to move.

But she couldn't. She was rooted to the spot by a mind-numbing panic that barely allowed her to suck in a breath. The guns. She wasn't usually rendered useless by the sight of guns. She'd shot her fair share, sometimes even carried one, and had been in the presence of them her whole life.

But these were so big, and they looked more military than recreational. She was sure she and Dylan were dead where they stood, and all the fight she was so certain she had in spades deserted her.

"Who are you?" one of the men demanded, gesturing his gun toward her. "Supposed to be one," he muttered to the other man. "Boss promised us it'd be one."

"What have you done to Adele?" Dylan asked.

Dylan's calmness was downright creepy. He didn't shake or seem panicked. Vanessa managed to keep a decent mask of not freaking out on the outside, but Dylan didn't seem to be acting. Easily, he stepped toward the two men, even as they aimed their guns at him.

Vanessa tried to swallow down the labored breathing that threatened to make too much noise in the quiet hall. She tried to move, but her body was still lead weight.

"Put the guns down and we'll make sure this ends well for everyone," Dylan said, still moving toward them, even as their fingers curled around the triggers. "Now, what have you done with my employee?"

Vanessa couldn't catch a breath. She and Dylan were going to die here in this hallway. Not just them, but their baby too. Her balance swayed and she had to squeeze her eyes shut and lean against the wall to find it again.

"Take them both?" one man asked the other.

The other seemed to consider it. "Only set up for one."

"Tricky business. Shoot her?"

Some awful sound escaped her throat, and she couldn't open her eyes or breathe. She was going to die. Her baby was going to die. Dylan was going to die.

Fight. You have to fight.

"Boss's got space. Rather take them both than get any blood on our hands till we know we can get away with it."

"Wasn't supposed to be two here. Boss's fault if we have to kill her."

Vanessa opened her eyes. She was still unaccountably dizzy, but she had to fight. For her baby. For herself. *Dylan.* "Are you seriously discussing whether or not to kill someone in front of said someone? What kind of criminals are you?" Vanessa demanded.

"Yeah, we'll take her," the bigger one sneered.

"Over my dead body," Dylan seethed, moving forward.

"I can arrange that," the sneering man said, jabbing the barrel of his gun right into Dylan's chest.

Vanessa went cold all over, even as she couldn't work out why Dylan was trying to save *her.* Just the baby, she supposed. Her teeth were chattering now, and she berated herself for being such a coward, but that didn't help give her the strength to push off the wall. To do anything. She could only stand here, shaking, falling apart, wondering why everything was spinning around her.

Except Dylan's profile. Something clicked off

in his expression. It wasn't fear that overtook him, even though this huge, monstrous weapon was pressed to his heart. It was…determination.

"You should leave her. She's pregnant. You don't want to mess with that. I'm the son of the bank president. Think of the ransom you could ask for. You don't need her, and you don't need to hurt her." Then Dylan did the damnedest thing. He smiled.

"Dylan," Vanessa managed. The hallway seemed to be getting dim, and she thought maybe she was going to throw up. She tried to say something, warn somebody that it wasn't going to be pretty. But the world was moving. The walls. The floor.

"Pregnant, eh?" One of the men eyed her and she had to close her eyes again. She had to think of the baby. If she could get her brain to stop being a jumbled mess, get the panic to stop freezing her, she could barricade herself in Dylan's office and call 911.

These men would be able to shoot through the glass door though. She'd left her cell phone in her car. Did Dylan have his on him? He seemed like the type who wouldn't be parted from it. She opened her eyes, trying to study his pants to see if there was the hint of a phone in his pocket.

"She's a liability," Dylan said, still so damn calm while she was shaking. Had the lights gone out? Everything seemed so dark. "Any harm you cause her would come back on you tenfold. It's one thing to kidnap and demand ransom, another to harm a woman and her unborn child."

"Only if we get caught," the other man said, his smile going so wide half his mouth was hidden behind his black face mask.

Vanessa thought she could all but read Dylan's thoughts from the simple murderous expression he gave the man: *oh, you'll be caught.*

She'd never given Dylan much credit for bravery or having a backbone, but watching him face down two goons with giant guns, she realized she had to reassess her opinion of him.

"We need to get going. We should have been gone ten minutes ago. Stick to the plan, or the boss—"

"Yeah, yeah, yeah." The man holding the gun to Dylan's chest pushed him with it. "You're coming with us." He gestured toward the back door Dylan had led her through not that long ago. Dylan started moving toward it, the gun now to his back.

He didn't even look at her as he passed.

"We can't leave her, pregnant or not. She's seen too much. We have to take her with us. Come on, little girl."

The man not pushing Dylan reached out for her, but she flinched away. She wanted to deck him, but she couldn't manage to move her arms. She couldn't *move*, period. Bile rose in her throat.

"I'm going to…" But the room was something like black, and she wasn't on her feet anymore. Then something crashed against her head and painful stars burst in her vision, but it wasn't light. She heard Dylan say her name, but she couldn't seem to do anything but stay still—and then float away.

DYLAN'S FACE THROBBED in time with his heavy beating heart. He should have been able to fight them off, but he'd been trying to get to Vanessa to make sure she was all right.

Now his hands were zip-tied behind his back, and he was pretty sure his shoulder was dislocated from trying to fight that off. It was possible his jaw was broken from the butt of the gun being smashed into his face, but since he could move it, he'd hope for just a severe bruise.

He'd never be able to break the bonds on his hands or feet, or even loosen them, but he kept feeling around the back of the van, trying to find something sharp.

Trying to keep his mind off the fact Vanessa was unconscious on the floor of the van and carrying his baby.

They'd been in the back of the vehicle for at

least fifteen minutes by his count, and Vanessa was still out cold. She was so pale. So…vulnerable.

He'd save her. He had to. His skills at survival had dulled somewhat these past few years of playing dutiful banker and protégé to his father. But he'd remember them. He'd bring them all back, and he and Vanessa would escape this mess.

Poor Adele. He hoped she was all right. Surely she'd have hit the alarm, even if they'd hurt her. But the two morons who'd abducted them had certainly taken their time getting out of the bank, and no one had shown up.

Well, someone would notice him missing. A Carson would surely notice Vanessa missing. Someone would notice she didn't come home and that her shop wasn't open. They'd see her car in the bank lot and know something was very, very wrong.

If he assured himself of those facts, he could concentrate on how they were going to escape. Because they *were* going to escape.

A quiet, gasping sound came from Vanessa's direction. Dylan scooted toward her. He wished he could maneuver himself to grab her hand, feel her pulse, but there wasn't enough room on the floor of the van.

"Vanessa."

She groaned this time, moving her head and then groaning again.

"Vanessa. Come on, sweetheart. Wake up." He tried nudging her with his elbow, but he couldn't lean that way without falling at every bump.

"Wh-what…?" She jerked at her arms, her legs thrashing wildly.

"Calm down. It's okay. I'm here. It's okay."

She jerked her gaze to him, all vicious anger hiding a little flash of fear. "Why would *you* being here make anything okay, Delaney?" she demanded, her voice rough. She looked around wildly.

"Just try to breathe. You fainted. Take your time to wake up. Then I'll help you sit up as best I can."

She sucked in a breath then let it out, eyeing their surroundings. The back of the van was all metal, and though the windows were tinted completely black, enough light shone through that they could make each other out. She moved her gaze to him.

"Fainted?" She tugged at the bonds on her hands as she moved herself into a sitting position—without his help—with a wince. "I've never fainted in my life."

"First time for everything. I'd imagine it had to do with—"

"How the hell am I tied up with *you* of all people?" She looked around, her expression one of panic with a steely disgust instead of that ashen terror from before. It was some comfort. "Where *are* we?"

"They took us both as hostages."

"Who's 'they'?" She pulled at the ties on her wrist again, then winced. She squeezed her eyes shut. "How did I get here? I can't…"

"What do you mean, 'you can't'?" He recalled that sometimes people with head injuries didn't remember what had caused them. Added to that, she'd fainted and suffered a trauma. Maybe she didn't even remember coming to see him at the bank. "You don't remember?"

"Remember what?" she snapped.

"What's the last thing you remember?"

She flashed him an impatient look, then her eyebrows drew together. "Man, someone did a number on your face." She seemed to finally understand he was tied up too.

"Yeah, yeah. We can talk about that later. Vanessa, what's the last thing you remember?"

She blinked, frowned. "I don't. Things are fuzzy around the edges. Fuzzy everywhere. I went to the grocery store this morning. Yeah." She closed her eyes and swallowed. "I'm not going to be sick," she muttered to herself, as if saying it aloud would make it so.

"That'd be preferable."

She frowned at him, but the confusion dominated her expression. "You look different. Your face is different."

"Must be the impressive bruising."

"No. You have lines."

"Lines?"

"Around your eyes. Your mouth. And that's some suit. Are we in Bent?" She tried to peer out the window, but she was still sitting and it was too black to see out of. "You're supposed to be in college, aren't you? Somewhere out east. Yeah, that's what I heard."

"College?" Panic threatened. *College.* She was just a little confused. By over a decade.

"A fancy one, right? I certainly remember your dad bragging all over himself about it when I went to the store this morning. Dylan this. Dylan that. For my benefit. As if *I'd* be impressed."

"Vanessa. God." It was as jarring of a blow as the butt of the gun to his face had been. "What year do you think it is?"

"What kind of question is that? It's…" Her brow furrowed again, and she shook her head. "It's… I'm sure it's…" She looked up at him help-lessly. "What's wrong with me?"

"You fainted. And you hit your head. Things are jumbled, but they'll clear up." He said it far more confidently than he felt it. She'd lost over a decade. That little trickle of panic turned into a full-on frantic clawing, but he ruthlessly shoved it down.

She'd just woken up. She was disoriented. The past ten years would come back. Everything with the baby would be okay.

It had to be.

"Got a phone on you?" he asked, his last hope at getting a message to someone.

"Why would I have a phone on me?"

Dylan swallowed down the bubble of hysterical laughter that tried to escape. He wouldn't panic and he wouldn't be hysterical. She'd be fine. She'd have to be. Surely pregnant women fainted and were fine, even with a little memory loss. Women had survived life on the prairie and what-have-you and had had plenty of babies. Everything was going to be fine if he kept his mind calm, his body ready.

He'd been a soldier once. He could be a soldier again.

"Okay, no phone. Anything sharp?"

"There should be a knife in my boot, but I can't get it with my hands behind my back like this. Who took us? Why are we both tied up? I don't—"

"One thing at a time. Let's get free and then I'll explain everything." Hopefully. Maybe she'd remember once she fully woke up. He had to hope there really was a knife in her boot, and she wasn't remembering a knife in her boot from thirteen years ago. "Put your legs out."

She did as he instructed, straightening her legs out in front of her.

"Which boot?"

"Right. There's a slot for it behind the outside of my ankle." Dylan scooted forward, maneuvering himself so the hands tied behind him were close to her ankle. He'd have to kind of lean over her legs and brush up against her to get his hands anywhere near her boot.

It was uncomfortable and awkward, but the most important thing was finding the knife, if in fact she had one down there in the here and now.

She fidgeted just as he finally got his fingertips down the side of her boot. "This is weird," she complained.

"No weirder than what you don't remember," he muttered, concentrating on leaning this way and that and ignoring the sharp pain in his ribs where one of the goons had kicked him, and the fact his head was all but in her lap.

It took a lot of time, a lot of contorting and a hell of a lot of pain every time the van went over a bump, but he managed to pull the knife out of her boot.

He was sweating by the time it clattered to the floor of the van, but he didn't wait around to catch his breath. The sooner he got them out of their bonds, the better. He leaned back, managed to grasp the knife. In a few swift movements, he cut the zip tie off his wrists.

Sometimes military training did come in handy in the civilian world. He wouldn't have guessed.

He didn't take a second to enjoy the feeling of freedom, however. He shook off the plastic and immediately cut the one around his ankle, and then freed Vanessa.

"Well. You move…fast," she said, as if that surprised her. "You better not have gotten me roped into this, Delaney."

"Quite the opposite."

"Figures. Always blame a Carson." She rubbed at her wrists, then delicately touched her fingertips to the side of her temple. She winced. "Some blow to the head."

"You folded like a card table and hit the ground before anyone could do anything."

She scowled. "I find that story very hard to believe."

"Well, I didn't knock you around and then tie us both up. But someone with guns *did* tie us up, so we need to be quick about getting ourselves out of this mess." But before they could do what needed to be done, she needed to recall one very important thing.

"You don't remember why you came to see me?" he asked carefully.

"I'm assuming these goons had a gun to my head, because that's the only way I would ever voluntarily go to see you. Unless you were being tortured. And I was invited to watch."

"Nice." Dylan sighed. This was going to make everything so much more difficult, but he didn't have time to get his nose out of joint about it. "I need you to understand something, okay?" He took a deep breath. If she really didn't remember years' worth of stuff, he doubted she'd believe him. He doubted a lot of things, but he couldn't let her go running around thinking it was just her. "You're pregnant."

She barked out a laugh. "Uh-huh."

"I'm serious. That's why we're together. You came to tell me."

"And why would I tell you… Oh. No. No." She shook her head back and forth. "You really expect me to believe I slept with *you*?"

"We were very drunk."

She shook her head, eyes wide. "I don't believe it. There's not enough liquor in the world."

"Okay. Don't believe it. But I need you to understand you *are* pregnant, it's thirteen years later than you think it is and bank robbers have kidnapped us to get a ransom. But I'm going to get us out of this, and when we escape you have to do everything in your power to keep the baby growing inside of you safe."

She went pale at that, but they didn't have time to keep discussing. The van had been moving too long, too far, and they had to make a serious jump-and-run effort here. She had to believe it, even if she didn't want to.

"It can't *be*," she whispered, pressing her hand to her stomach.

"But it is."

Chapter Three

Vanessa didn't believe him. Maybe things were all wrong—from the lines on his face to the nausea in her gut to the van they were trapped in—but she would have never slept with Dylan Delaney, even with a blow to her head.

And *he* would have never slept with *her*.

Dylan was fiddling with the door, looking serious and in control. He'd been beaten up pretty badly, but he didn't seem to pay it any mind. He wore a suit—and even though it was dirty and rumpled, she could tell it was expensive.

Her eyes stung, and it took a few moments to realize she wanted to cry. Everything was wrong, like a bad dream where only half the things made sense, no matter how real it all felt.

But cry? Not her. Not in this lifetime. She blinked a few times, and focused on the here and now. Not anything Dylan was claiming, but the fact they were tied up in the back of a van, and now Dylan was using her knife and his bloody hands to mess with the door.

"Can I help?" she managed to ask once she could trust her voice.

"Just sit back."

She scowled. She wasn't a *sit-back* kind of girl, but she wouldn't have pegged Dylan as a take-charge kind of guy. Sure, to order people around maybe, but not to try and bust them out of a moving van.

How could this all be happening? She was about to demand he explain this and tell her the truth instead of his nonsense dream—lies—about her being pregnant with *his* baby.

She pressed a hand to her stomach, acknowledging that she *might* feel really off. But couldn't that just be the head injury? Couldn't Dylan have *caused* the head injury? Sure, he was all beat up, and he'd been tied up too, but…

She tried to remember. Tried to order her thoughts and memories, but the very last thing she remembered was flipping off Dylan's dad as she left the Delaney General Store.

Not her finest moment, but…

But nothing. The old jerk deserved it. She opened her eyes to the young Delaney jerk in front of her, still trying to jimmy the back door open. He didn't look right. He looked older. Was she really missing such a big chunk of time?

She looked down at her hands. There were pink marks and scratches where the zip ties had dug into her skin around her wrists, but otherwise her hands looked the same. Same rings she always wore... Well, maybe not exactly. She fiddled with a dainty-looking gold one in the shape of a mountain. She didn't remember that one.

She had to find some kind of center—both a mental one and a physical one. This weakness in both wouldn't save her, and it wouldn't fill in whatever memory blanks she had.

But the van chose that moment to rumble to a stop, followed by the engine shutting off.

Oh, God.

Dylan swore, then sat down on the floor of the van right by the doors. "Stand behind me," he ordered, like he knew what he was doing, like he could get them out of whatever this was. "Be ready to jump. On my signal, run as fast as you can for whatever cover you can find."

"What about you?" Not that she *cared* about Dylan, but...

He flashed her a grin so incongruous with the Dylan Delaney she'd grown up alongside, she could only gape at him.

The door made a noise, like a lock being undone. "Be ready," Dylan murmured, leaning back on his palms as he watched the door.

"What are you—"

The door began to open, and on an exhale Dylan kicked his legs out as hard as he could against the doors. There were twin grunts of pain as the doors hit something, but Dylan didn't pause. He flung the doors back open and jumped out.

"Go!" he instructed.

Because she saw one man on the ground, struggling to get to his feet, with a *huge* gun next to him, she did as Dylan instructed. She jumped out of the van and immediately started to run.

"Opposite way!" Dylan yelled. She turned, ready to do whatever Dylan instructed if it'd get her out of here, and watched in the fading dusk as his yell ended on a grunt as one of the large men landed an elbow to his gut.

Dylan Delaney, a hoity-toity Delaney who was getting a fancy degree and likely hadn't done an ounce of manual labor in his entire life, took the blow like it barely glanced off him. Then he pivoted, swept a leg out and knocked one large man on his butt. Dylan reared back a fist and punched the other guy in the throat, then whirled as the fallen man got back to his feet.

Vanessa blinked.

"Go!" Dylan yelled at her, and it got through her absolute shock at seeing him fight like he knew what he was doing. No, not even like he knew what he was doing. Like he was *born* to do it.

But there were angry men and guns, so she ran the opposite way she'd been going, toward the front of the van. It acted as a buffer between her and the men and gave her the opportunity to get away without them seeing exactly where she was going.

Dylan knew what he was doing—between the instruction to run this way and fighting off two men. What the hell? She shook away her confusion and focused on running as hard as she could. Her stomach lurched and her head throbbed, but the guns brought it home that she was running for her life here.

And your baby's life?

She couldn't think about Dylan's nonsense right now. She just had to get away. She ran hard, but the farther she ran, the darker it got. She had to slow her pace so she didn't trip. So she didn't throw up.

With heaving breaths, she slowed to a stop and pressed her hand to her stomach. She had a cramp in her side that felt like a sharp icepick. When she stopped, she was nearly felled by a nasty wave of nausea. Her head downright ached, and the stinging behind her eyes was back.

But she was in danger, and a Carson knew how to get herself out of danger. She swallowed at the sickness threatening, focused on evening her breath, then studied her surroundings.

She had run for the trees—the best cover she could find—but they were spindly aspens, and it wasn't ideal to be hiding behind even a cluster of narrow trunks. The van must have driven them up in elevation, but where? It was completely dark now, and she couldn't get a sense of her bearings.

Panic joined the swirl of queasiness in her stomach. She breathed through both. She could survive a night in the wild. She didn't particularly *care* to, but she could survive. As long as Dylan had taken care of those two armed men, she was safe enough. Anyone could brave the elements for one night.

And if Dylan didn't fight them off?

It was hard to imagine it. He'd moved like a dancer. A really violent, potentially lethal dancer. Dylan Delaney. She would have labeled him the prissiest of the four Delaney kids. Even his younger sister Jen had more spitfire to her than Dylan.

But he was claiming they'd slept together, that he'd impregnated her somehow, and then she'd watched him fight like a dream.

Touching fingertips to the bump on her head, where everything throbbed and ached, Vanessa had to wonder if the blow had caused hallucinations.

Either way, she was alone in the dark in the

middle of the Wyoming woods. She lowered herself to the ground, leaning her back against one of the rough trees. It was uncomfortable, and a chill was creeping into the air.

It would be fine. There wasn't snow on the ground, and the leaves still clung to the trees, though they'd gone gold in a nod to fall. But they hadn't completely fallen.

Luckily, she was too nauseous to be hungry, though she wouldn't mind a drink of water. But she'd live. She was alive, and she'd live.

"There you are."

She would have screamed if a hand hadn't clamped over her mouth. She turned her head to find herself face-to-face with Dylan. It was too dark to make out the individual features of his face, and yet she knew it was him.

"Shh. Okay?"

She nodded and his hand fell off her mouth.

"What happened? How are you… How am I… What is going *on*?"

Breathing only a little heavily, he scanned the dark. "I managed to incapacitate one."

"Incapaci-what?"

"I didn't have time to incapacitate the other," he continued, clearly not worried about how odd his word choice was. "Figured I had a better chance to catch up with you so we're armed."

And he *had* caught up with her.

He'd fought off two armed men like he belonged in some sort of action spy movie, run fast enough to catch up with her and now, in his rumpled, torn suit, was holding a giant semiautomatic weapon as if he knew how to use it.

"Who *are* you?"

He flashed her that incongruous grin again, just barely visible in the night around them. "Well, clearly not who you think I am."

THEY WERE IN TROUBLE. Dylan would be less worried about being stuck he wasn't quite sure where in the dark if Vanessa wasn't pregnant and sporting a hell of a head injury. He couldn't let himself dwell on that too much. All he stood to lose.

No, a good soldier focused on the mission at hand, not the future.

He hadn't had a chance to put his real talents to use, he thought bitterly as he looked at the gun. Knocking out the first guy and getting his weapon had taken more time than Dylan cared to admit, and when the second guy had hopped into the van and tried to run him down, Dylan's best choice had been to run, not shoot like the sniper he'd been once upon a time.

"I need an explanation," Vanessa said, and he

knew she wanted to sound strong and demanding, but he heard the tremor of fear in her voice.

How had this day gone so far to hell so fast?

"I don't really have one," he said softly. None of this made sense to him. A bank robbery was foolish, but they'd gotten away with it. Except they hadn't taken any money. They'd taken him and Vanessa.

"More of one than I do."

Dylan sighed. He couldn't see well in the dark, but he was fairly the certain the other man had lost him in the trees where his van couldn't follow and headlights couldn't penetrate deep enough.

Still, Dylan needed to be on alert until morning. Maybe with daylight he'd be able to figure out where they were and get them home.

Surely someone knew something was wrong at this point, with both him and Vanessa missing, Vanessa's car in the bank's parking lot. Adele was likely hurt—he had to accept that more-than-possibility, and she didn't have anyone waiting for her at home. But maybe she wasn't fatally hurt and—

"Dylan. Answers." Vanessa gritted her teeth, and he wondered if it was to keep them from chattering.

"Still no memory, then?"

She was silent for a few moments, except for the rustling of her fidgeting. "No. I… No. My last memory is that morning in the store with your dad, but if I try to come up with a year or how old I am, it all jumbles up. Some things make sense and some don't." Her voice trembled at the end, and she didn't say more.

"You seem to be missing about a decade. More than, actually. I've been home from…college for ten years."

"Why'd you pause all weird before you said *college*?"

"I didn't," he replied, irritated that she'd picked up on that. "Now, can we focus on the here and now?"

"I have *amnesia* and lost ten years plus off my life and you—"

"Just fought off two armed men who wanted to kick us around and use us for ransom. In the best-case scenario. Now we're alone in the woods with no supplies or help. Do you have any idea where we are?"

"It's too dark. It's too…"

He wouldn't let her panic, so he spoke over her. "The way I figure it we drove south out of town, and kept on that way since the sun was setting into the window when we left. That puts us close to Carson territory. Maybe."

"Maybe. But none of this looks familiar to me."

"That's okay. We don't want to be moving around in the night anyway. In the morning we'll have a better idea." One way or another. "How are you feeling?"

"Am I really…?" She paused, then audibly swallowed.

"Pregnant? As far as I know. You came by the bank to tell me. That's when these men came in. I hope they didn't kill Adele." He muttered the last to himself. "I was too hard on her. Sharp mind, abrasive attitude, sure, but she was always a stellar employee. I should have…" Not the mission at hand though. He blew out a breath. "You need to rest. Tomorrow might be a bit of a rough day. We'll have a lot of walking to do."

He moved from a crouch to a seated position next to her. He positioned the gun so he was able to hold it and wrap his free arm around her shoulders.

She tensed and leaned away. "What are you doing?" she demanded.

"Being your makeshift pillow, sweetheart."

"You think I'm going to sleep on you?" She sounded so horrified it gave him some semblance of hope.

"You may not remember, but you've done a lot worse on me."

She recoiled, and he couldn't help but chuckle. "If it helps, on that front, I don't remember either. It is no exaggeration that the night we were together was the drunkest I've ever been. Some-

where during the reception my mind goes black."
Maybe he had a few flashes here and there of soft
sighs or the silk of her hair, but she didn't need
to know that.

She didn't lean into him, but she'd stopped
leaning away. "I…"

"It's going to be a chilly night. We'll keep each
other warm. Hopefully, you catch a few hours
sleep. We move at first light. No ulterior mo-
tives. Just common sense and getting through
this…ordeal."

"Are they going to come after us?"

Dylan wanted to lie, to reassure her. It was
strange to want to comfort Vanessa, but she
wasn't herself. She was pregnant. With a bump on
her head. And amnesia. She was a mess, and everything in him had softened completely at that.

Still, it was important she knew what they were
up against. "I have no idea. Which is why you
need to sleep, and I'll keep watch."

"Don't you need to sleep?"

"I'll be just fine."

She leaned into him, slowly, almost incre-
mentally. Eventually, her head rested against his
shoulder.

It felt oddly comforting.

"Where did you learn to fight?" she asked, her
voice thick with exhaustion.

Briefly, he wondered if he should keep her

awake because of concussion concerns, but she needed rest. She was *pregnant*. And they had no food or water. Surely rest was better, and it wasn't like they'd get much anyway.

He didn't answer her question, and when she didn't push, he figured she'd fallen asleep.

Funny, Vanessa was one of the few people who probably wouldn't be horrified by where he'd learned to fight, by all the lies he'd told. She'd love it.

She'd also tell his family with relish and glee, regardless of the accidental pregnancy.

Why that made him want to smile in the middle of this mess, he didn't have a clue.

Chapter Four

Back in Bent

Laurel Delaney parked her police cruiser in front of Delaney Bank and glanced at the man in the passenger seat.

Deputy Hart didn't know it yet, but she'd asked him to be her second on this call because soon enough she'd have to disclose her pregnancy to her superiors. They might let her continue to do some light detective work but not in the field. Desk duty. *Ugh.*

Regardless of how she felt at having to sit things out for *months*, Hart would be a good replacement for the duration of her desk duty and maternity leave. Yet that didn't make it easy to accept someone else taking the role she'd worked so hard for. Bent County only had one detective spot, and she loved it.

Sometimes you sacrificed what you loved for who you loved. She may have only just found out about this baby, but she already loved the child she and Grady had created with everything she was.

Which was why Hart would take the lead on this case. Probably best regardless of her physical condition, considering the man who'd called it in was her father.

Dad stood in front of the bank, looking grave and irritated. His patented look.

He didn't know about the pregnancy yet— no one but her and Grady did at this point. Dad wouldn't be happy. But then, nothing about his children's choices of significant others lately made him happy. Dylan and Jen were his only hopes. Laurel and Cam had been relegated to black sheep at best due to their choice to connect their lives with Carsons.

It hadn't been a choice, falling in love with Grady. Though she supposed they'd chosen to center their lives in that love.

Laurel sighed and gave Deputy Hart a thin smile. "I'd ask you to take the lead, but my dad is only going to want to deal with me."

Hart grinned. Laurel knew he cursed his baby face, but she thought it'd often work in his favor as a detective. People underestimated the sharp mind and conscientious attention to detail underneath. "I'm counting on it," he offered cheerfully.

Laurel rolled her eyes but got out of her car.

Darkness had settled around the bank, but the lights were still on. She took a deep breath of fresh air and shored up her patience to deal with her father.

"Dad."

"Laurel." He didn't even give Hart a cursory look. "Took you long enough."

"You said it wasn't an emergency."

Dad merely shrugged. "Have you heard from Dylan?"

"No, but I wasn't expecting to. Why don't you tell me what you think happened?"

"I don't know what happened," Dad snapped. He smoothed out his features, clearly remembering that it wasn't just her in his audience. He had to play the role of upstanding Delaney for Deputy Hart. "I was driving home from the airport after my meeting in Denver. I passed the bank and saw the normal lights on instead of the security lights. So I pulled in, thinking someone had forgotten to switch over to closing lights, but the door was unlocked and no one was inside."

"And you suspect foul play?"

Dad pressed his lips together, a sure sign of irritation. "I don't know what to suspect. Neither your brother nor Adele will answer their phones. The safes are all closed and locked, and nothing appears out of place, but the evening paperwork wasn't done, so I can't be sure if every dollar is accounted for."

"So it was just Adele and Dylan working?" She nodded at Hart to start taking notes, pleased to see he already was. He was going to be a good replacement. Just hopefully not so good she couldn't get her detective spot back when she returned from maternity leave.

But that was so far away. She didn't need to think about it now.

"As far as I know. Adele was scheduled to close. Dylan wasn't scheduled, but it's not unheard of for him to be here until close. Still, we didn't have any meetings, and he tends to check in with the foreman at the ranch before the foreman's done at five."

"Why don't Hart and I take a look around? Have you been home to see if Dylan's there?"

"No, but I called George and he hadn't seen him."

Laurel felt the first little tickle of worry at the base of her spine. "Hart, I'll take the inside. You take the outside. Dad, do you have security tapes?"

He puffed out his chest. "Of course. I haven't had a chance to look at them. I called you once I realized my bank had been abandoned and unlocked for who knows how long."

"Pull up the footage," Laurel instructed, stepping inside. She began to look around the front counter. Though she'd never planned on following her father's footsteps at the bank, she'd spent some time working as a part-time teller when she'd been in the police academy, since Dad had refused to pay for that.

She knew her way around, and nothing appeared out of place. It didn't look like your typical burglary. Surely it had just been someone's mistake. She couldn't imagine her brother or Adele Oscar, one of Dad's higher-up employees, being that careless. But maybe if there'd been an emergency elsewhere?

Yet there was the gut feeling that had gotten her through her years as a deputy, and now as Bent County Sheriff's Department's detective, that told her something was off. That this was more than an oversight.

Hart appeared at the front doors. "There are two cars in the employee lot out back," he said. "You want to come see if you recognize them?"

Laurel nodded and motioned Hart to follow her through the back hall that would cut through the bank to the back lot. She passed Dad's office and stopped when she saw him scowling and punching at the computer keys.

He looked up and, though his face was scowling and angry, she saw the hint of worry in his gaze. "I'm not sure what happened, but there's no footage today. It appears the cameras were turned off last night."

"Purposeful?"

Dad shrugged. "I don't know. I suppose it could be an accident, but whoever did it had access."

"I'll need a list of anyone who has access and opportunity to turn on or off the cameras. Hart, sit down with him and write down everyone who had access. I'm going to check out the cars." She moved through the back hallway briskly, that gut feeling diving deeper.

She immediately recognized the first vehicle, her brother's sleek sports car. It was enough to make her feel uneasy. Why would Dylan have left his car behind? Still, she could have come up with a few reasons. But the second car, parked farther down, made her stomach flip over in absolute police-level concern.

What was Vanessa Carson's car doing in the Delaney Bank parking lot? That wasn't just abnormal—it was unheard of.

Laurel immediately pulled out her phone. When the rough voice answered, the noise of his saloon a steady hum behind him, she couldn't smile like she usually did. "Grady."

"What's up, princess?"

The nickname didn't bug her anymore, but this feeling did. "Have you seen Vanessa today?"

"Van? Hmm. Guess not, but I wasn't expecting to." There was a pause. "What is it?"

"I'm not sure. Can you send someone to see if she's at her shop and give me a call back?"

"Laurel, do I need to be worried?"

It was her turn to pause. "I'm not sure."

"But you are. Worried, that is."

"Call me back, okay? Love you."

"Laur—"

She couldn't sit on the phone and argue with her husband. She marched back inside to her father's office. "It's Dylan's car and Vanessa Carson's."

Hart's eyebrows rose and Dad's face turned a mottled red.

"Are you telling me—"

"I'm telling you those are the cars left in the lot, and both people are unaccounted for. We need to find Adele Oscar. If she was working, and her car's gone, we need her story. If she won't answer her phone, we'll have to go find her."

Hart nodded. Laurel looked at her father. "Lock up. Go home. I'll let you know when I've got more information."

"I demand—"

"Go home, Dad. Let us investigate." She pushed Hart toward the front doors and to the police car.

She had a bad feeling Adele Oscar had something to do with this weirdness. Now they just had to find her.

Chapter Five

Vanessa awoke to a barrage of bad feelings. Pain, sharp and relentless, in her head and against her eyes. A roiling queasiness that seemed more familiar than not. Hunger. And a nasty crick in her neck.

She groaned in protest as her bed seemed to move out from under her. When she opened her eyes against the warm glow of sunrise, she realized she wasn't lying on a bed. She was on the cold, hard ground, curled around and tangled up in a very warm and comfortable Dylan Delaney.

He was staring at her, and she could only stare back, because if she moved she would throw up.

There was a prickle at the base of her spine, and a warm wave of…something low in her stomach.

His eyes were dark brown, closer to black. Had she ever noticed that before? He had the scrape of a five-o'clock shadow, which still didn't hide that sharp cut of his jaw. She had the insane urge to touch her fingers to his cheek to see if the bristle of whiskers would be as rough as it looked, if his cheekbones were really that sharp.

It was something elemental inside her, as if she simply belonged here and he belonged there. She should touch him because he was hers, looking dangerous almost. Like a pirate or an outlaw out of time. As if he'd whisk her away and she'd never fight back, because this was exactly—

Dylan Delaney? Dangerous? Her not fight back? What a laugh. She was clearly delirious.

"It's morning," she managed to say when he didn't move or say anything, just kept staring at her with dark eyes that seemed to go on forever, a century of secrets and longing.

Some bump on the head she had.

"That it is." Carefully, with a gentleness that touched her even though it shouldn't, he disentangled himself and got to his feet. Then he held out a hand and pulled her up.

She closed her eyes against the wave of nausea, tried to swallow against her cottony mouth.

"You don't look so good."

She wanted to be insulted, but she felt way worse than that.

"I want you to stay here," Dylan instructed.

Normally, instructions got her back up, especially delivered by a high-and-mighty Delaney, but there was something about his that made her feel safe.

"I'm going to find some water," he continued. "You stay put and look around and think about if anything looks familiar, okay? The gun is right there if you need it."

Again, some part of her brain insisted she argue with him, but it was buried deep underneath a fog of exhaustion. "Okay."

He nodded and headed off for the pines.

"Wait. How will you find your way back?"

His mouth curved, that ironic twist of humor she had yet to figure out. "I'll manage."

She wanted to believe he was stupid. That he'd get lost and she'd be left alone. That'd be preferable, wouldn't it? Fending for herself rather than teaming up with a Delaney.

But as he disappeared, panic bubbled in her chest. Just about any company was better than no company in this particular situation.

She tried to focus on the task he'd given her. Find something familiar. But the aspens and pines and rocks could be any in Bent County.

The sky was blue, the sun slowly warming up the air. Maybe they weren't even in Bent County. Maybe they weren't even in *Wyoming*.

She wrapped her arms around herself, trying to squeeze away the panic.

Would she know where she was if she wasn't

missing chunks of time? She closed her eyes, trying to work through the years that were apparently missing.

But all she saw was Dylan's face. The dark whiskers, his dark eyes. Something lurking behind them that called to something inside of her. A certainty and a calmness that steadied her when she wanted to fall apart.

She didn't want him to find his way back, or so she told herself, but she knew he would. She was certain he'd return with water and that enviable certainty.

She was hungry and thirsty and *insane*. She opened her eyes, shook away Dylan's face and focused on survival.

He was going to find some water. Even if his crazy story about her being pregnant was true, she could survive a few days without food. But she needed water.

She sucked a breath in, then out, finding deep breaths helped the queasiness.

Pregnant. She placed a hand over her stomach, trying to divine if there was any truth to it. Sure, queasiness could be morning sickness, but couldn't it also be the aftereffects of the blow to the head? Couldn't that account for the exhaustion, as well?

Wouldn't she know on some deep maternal level if there was a human being growing inside her? She didn't know. She didn't feel certain either way.

But why would Dylan make up this ridiculous story about being the father of her supposed unborn baby? He wouldn't want that, even as a joke. Even if she was missing chunks of time, there was no way her feelings about Dylan, or his about her, had changed so drastically either of them would want to be parents together.

She gingerly touched a finger to the knot on her head, then winced at the pain from even the lightest touch.

Everything was so messed up, and instead of being her usual alert, tough, kick-butt self, she felt like a blob of uselessness.

She leaned against the tree, then went ahead and slid to the ground so she was sitting next to the gun Dylan had propped against it. What could she do but sit here and wait? Cry? She certainly wanted to, but she'd never let a Delaney see her cry if she could help it.

So she breathed. She kept looking around the small clearing trying to find something familiar, and she waited. She listened for footsteps and Dylan's return, but she heard nothing except wind and occasionally the faint sounds of scurrying.

Something puttered nearby. Wait. Was that a car? Definitely an engine. Slowly, Vanessa got to her feet. She began to follow the noise, leaving herself a trail to get back to the clearing, because she knew a thing or two about not getting lost in the woods or mountains.

It didn't take her long to get to what appeared to be a road. Dirty and bumpy. Clearly not used often, but similar to the one that ran up to the Carson cabin. Again, she looked around. She wasn't near her family's cabin, she didn't think, but they were definitely in the mountains. Isolated.

And then, almost as if she were walking through a dream, a car appeared. A sleek sedan, so out of place in the rough yet breathtaking Wyoming mountains. She *was* in Wyoming. Somewhere close to home. She had to believe that.

The sedan rolled to a stop, and the tinted driver's-side window slid down. The woman's face behind the steering wheel didn't look familiar. Vanessa squinted at her, searching for some kind of recognition.

"Hello there." The woman smiled, though it struck Vanessa as too sharp for friendliness.

"Hi."

"You seem…" The woman trailed off and looked around. "Lost. Alone."

"I'm not alone."

"Oh?"

Something about the way the woman jumped on that made Vanessa nervous, and really made her wish she'd thought to bring the gun. Silly. What could this woman do to her? She was help. Salvation maybe.

"We are lost though. Do you have a phone so I could call someone we know to come get us?" If she remembered anyone's number—the ranch. She knew the number to the ranch. Surely that hadn't changed, if it had really been years since she could remember. Noah or Ty would help her.

"I'm afraid it doesn't have any service up here." The woman's expression changed, but Vanessa couldn't read it. There was an element of sheepishness to the shrug, but it was too...pointed.

Vanessa took a step back from the car.

"I can give you a ride back to town," the woman offered. "If that's where you want to go. I was headed up to my cabin, but you look like you need some help."

Vanessa glanced back at the pines. She could take the offer, and then send someone back to get Dylan. Surely it'd be the smart, rational thing to do. Wasn't she positive Dylan could take care of himself?

"What town?"

The woman cocked her head. "Are you okay?"

"Could you wait?" she asked, wincing at her own idiocy. "I just need to get the man I'm stranded with."

The woman studied her. "You've got quite the

bump on your face. You sure you want to get him, Vanessa?"

"He had nothing— You know me."

The woman's eyebrows drew together. "Of course I know you. I know we're not exactly *friends* or anything, but I've lived in Bent since I took a job at the bank."

Vanessa took another step back. Her instincts were all off, but this felt wrong. Of course Dylan Delaney felt right, which *had* to be wrong.

Nothing made sense. Nothing. The mention of the bank made her stomach clench—not in its normal disdainful way when faced with anything having to do with Delaneys either. Something closer to fear.

"You're hurt," the woman said, and though her voice itself was gentle, something in the tone was harsh, grating. "And scared. Let me take you into town. To Rightful Claim. Oh, wait, your brother doesn't live there anymore, does he?"

"I…" Grady. Grady didn't live above Rightful Claim anymore? The saloon he ran was his heart and soul. Where would he have gone? The Carson ranch, maybe. She opened her mouth to ask, but then decided better of it. She didn't know this woman, and no matter what she knew about Vanessa, she gave her an uncomfortable feeling. Vanessa had never been one for parading her weaknesses to strangers, and this weird memory loss was quite the weakness.

She might be all messed up in the head, but she'd always trusted her uncomfortable gut feelings before. Head injury or not, some form of amnesia or not, she had to trust her internal feelings of right and wrong.

"Vanessa!"

It was Dylan's voice. She wanted to run toward it, no matter how little sense that made. "Hold on," she mumbled to the woman. She walked back the way she'd come. "Dylan! I found a road."

It only took a few minutes before Dylan appeared, something like fury dug into the lines in his face. Until he saw the car. He rushed toward it.

"Adele."

That name rang some bell deep underneath the fog in Vanessa's brain, but the woman's face still didn't. But Dylan knew her. Maybe Vanessa should be relieved.

But all she could feel was regret he hadn't grabbed the gun she'd left behind.

"You're all right," Dylan said to the woman, coming to a stop just a few paces in front of the car. Surprise and then something like suspicion flashed over his face. He glanced at Vanessa, then back to the driver.

"We're just worried sick, Dylan," the woman

said, suddenly sounding scared and just that. Worried sick. "What on earth happened?"

Vanessa frowned at the woman. She'd changed her tune now that Dylan was here. Put on this little panicked act. She hadn't been at all panicked or surprised before.

Vanessa didn't buy it for a second. "I—"

"You'll drive us back into town, then," Dylan said with that commanding tone of voice that made Vanessa want to roll her eyes. *Men*. Delaney men at that.

But he hadn't grabbed the gun and this felt all wrong. He needed to know, to see something wasn't right. "Dylan—"

He was already opening the car door to the back seat. "Adele will drive us back to town." He took Vanessa's arm, pulling her to the car. "She works for me at the bank. She'll get us back."

"Dylan," Vanessa hissed as he pushed her gently into the back seat. "I don't think—"

He slid inside next to her. "To the hospital, Adele. Vanessa needs to be checked out."

"Of course."

Vanessa didn't trust the odd smile Adele flashed into the rearview mirror, but she kept her mouth shut.

DYLAN FIDGETED—SOMETHING he almost never did. But the fact Adele was safe and whole, and here, struck him as wrong. It had all his senses on high alert, waiting for trouble.

Beggars couldn't be choosers though, and Vanessa needed a hospital, enough so he didn't think it prudent to wait to go retrieve the gun he had left. Once he got Vanessa checked out, he'd be talking to Laurel about what had happened anyway.

Besides, what could one middle-aged woman do to the two of them? He didn't consider himself invincible or anything, but two-against-one odds were already in his favor. Add his military training and he was sure they were good, even if she had a weapon.

Weapon? Adele? This was ridiculous. What reason would Adele have to hurt them? She'd worked for Delaney Bank for over a decade and slowly worked her way up the ladder. She could be a little harsh and abrasive, but she did her work meticulously. She was devoted to the bank, which he'd always assumed meant she was devoted to the Delaneys.

"Lucky thing you two were on the road up to the cabin I rented for my vacation," Adele said. "Not sure what might have happened to you if I hadn't come along. Fate sure is a funny thing."

"You weren't scheduled for a vacation," Dylan said. Though Adele was technically in charge of creating the schedule, Dylan oversaw it. Knew it by heart. It was a habit he'd been taught by his father. *Always know who's in charge of what.* Dad did it to lord mistakes over people. Dylan had never been comfortable with that reason, but he made sure to know nonetheless. He never knew what that made him.

"Oh, I worked it out with your father," Adele said, her voice still overly cheerful. Not like her, and not at all appropriate for the situation.

Worse, as she drove she kept climbing the mountain. She didn't ask any questions about why they were wandering around the mountains lost, or why he had bruises on his face or why Vanessa had a bump on her head and needed a hospital.

Dylan realized far too late his worry over Vanessa's—and the baby's—health had caused him to make a very rash decision.

But this was Adele. He'd worked with Adele since he'd come back to Bent. It wasn't like they were best friends or anything, but he knew her. He and his dad had trusted her with all manner of bank business. Surely his instincts were going haywire because he was worried, because he was confused.

Because Vanessa Carson had dropped the bomb that she was pregnant with his child minutes before they'd been kidnapped. Of course things didn't feel right. None of this was right.

But he couldn't convince himself this gnawing

pit of doom opening up in his gut was something other than a premonition.

"Town's the opposite way," he noted. Not because he knew where they were, but because he knew going *up* the mountain definitely wasn't heading toward any town.

"Nowhere to turn around yet. Be patient." She flicked him a glance in the rearview mirror. "Isn't that what your father is always saying? 'Patience, Adele,'" she said, the last two words a low imitation of his father's voice.

Then she laughed.

Dylan didn't dare look at Vanessa, but with an unerringness that surprised even him, he found her hand and curled his around it. He could feel the tension radiating off her. She might not remember Adele with a portion of her memory missing, but she could feel how wrong this all was too.

And it was his fault. This whole thing from top to bottom. He couldn't even work up the righteous anger that Vanessa hadn't listened to him back at the bank and stayed in his office. He wouldn't have. How could he have expected her to?

Now they were in danger. No matter how he tried to convince himself he could handle Adele and that she wasn't out to get them, every cell of his being screamed otherwise.

She finally pulled up in front of a cabin. It

looked like a fairly new construction and was completely isolated. It wasn't part of a cluster of cabins rented out to the odd tourist, and it wasn't like the Carson cabin, a ramshackle nod to the past.

"Adele. She needs a hospital," Dylan said calmly, clearly, keeping Vanessa's hand in his. He could overtake Adele. Drive Vanessa himself. He didn't want to hurt Adele, but he could, and he would if it meant getting Vanessa help. Getting their baby help.

Adele pushed the car into Park and then gave the horn a little honk. She looked over her shoulder at him, looking vaguely sympathetic. "I know. I really am sorry about this whole thing."

"Adele…"

But he trailed off when she pointed to the door of the cabin. His heart sank when the two men who'd kidnapped them stepped out. One still with his gun, the other bandaged and holding a rifle. Both unmasked this time around.

Hell.

Chapter Six

Vanessa could only stare at the two burly men
standing in the doorway. This was bad. Still, with
Dylan holding her hand in his larger one, she felt
safe.

You are so very not safe, moron.

Adele turned around to face them, and this
time her expression was one of pure contrition.
Vanessa didn't know why she didn't believe it,
but she flat out didn't.

"I'm so sorry," Adele said, keeping her gaze
on Dylan. "I had to," she whispered.

"You had to what?" Dylan demanded, his voice
sharp as a blade. It made Vanessa shiver. No matter how uncharacteristic this was of the Dylan she
knew, or thought she knew, she wouldn't cross
this man.

Apparently, Adele had no problems doing so
though. "They told me I had to find you, and I
had to bring you back to them. They threatened
my life. I didn't have a choice."

"A choice? You were in a car by yourself! You could have gone to town and—"

She shook her head sadly. "You don't understand, Dylan. I'm afraid you're going to have to go along with this. Now, don't worry. They assured me they won't hurt us. A ransom is all they're after. We just have to do what they say."

"Why didn't they hurt you?" Vanessa demanded. Both Dylan and Adele blinked over at her. But the fact of the matter was, Adele was unscathed and she and Dylan were not.

"I went along with everything they said," Adele replied, a slight edge to her voice. It softened with her next words though. "If we all do, we get out of this alive."

"How can you be so sure?"

"So far, so good. Come on, get out before they drag you out." Adele looked at Vanessa. "We wouldn't want that, would we?" As if she knew Vanessa was pregnant.

How would she know? Surely she couldn't divine that simply from Dylan saying she needed a hospital.

Adele got out of the driver's seat and held up her hands as she walked over to the two men, as if in surrender. Then all three of them watched Dylan and Vanessa climb out of the car.

"None of this adds up," Vanessa muttered as

they stood, almost in a face-off with the men a few yards away.

"No. It doesn't," Dylan agreed. "But for the time being, Adele is right. If we play along, they won't hurt us." He nudged her gently forward.

Vanessa gave a pointed look at all the wounds on his face as they trudged their way toward the cabin.

He shrugged. "A few bruises won't kill me. They'll have food and water. Shelter. A ransom requires keeping us alive. Right now, since we can't get medical attention, getting you food and water is the most important thing. If this is dangerous, I'll find a way to get us out. For the time being, you'll get to rest and be cared for."

It was very strange to have someone looking out for her. Oh, she had a big brother and two cousins who'd lay down their lives for hers. But they weren't the fussy sort. None of the Carsons were. They'd protect and defend, but they wouldn't think to put getting her rest above their other objectives.

"Good job delaying the inevitable," one of the men said with a happy grin. "Welcome home, friends." He was covered in bandages, clearly the man Dylan had "incapacitated."

Vanessa didn't like the gleam in his eye. Not out of fear for herself but fear for Dylan. It didn't matter that she *hated* Dylan, and she was sure she did. Once this was all over and her memory returned, the hate would come back and everything would make sense. She wouldn't care about Dylan's well-being at all.

But in that car he'd held her hand. In this short walk to the men waiting for them with gleaming smiles and guns, he'd expressed concern over her well-being.

Because she was pregnant. Allegedly. And the baby was his. Supposedly. That must have been why he felt the need to take care of her. If it was all true, he was only protecting what was his.

Vanessa was unaccountably tired all of a sudden. She even swayed on her feet against her will. But Dylan held her up.

A Delaney held her up. She couldn't believe what was happening.

"She needs a place to rest. Water. Food."

"Don't recall you being the one in charge here, friend," the man with the bandages said to Dylan. "Best you remember that before we do another number on your face."

"Seems like he did a number on you," Vanessa muttered before she thought better of it.

"Boss didn't say anything about you pulling in a hefty ransom. You might be useless to us."

Dylan stepped forward, even as the barrel of both weapons pointed at him. "You lay one hand on her, you'll pay in every possible way for a man to pay. I don't care how many guns you point at me."

Something poked through the fog in her brain. That same image of Dylan facing down deadly weapons but in a different place.

Adele laughed nervously, and the image skittered away. "Wh-why don't we all calm down? No one wants to get hurt." Dylan spared her a glance that would have melted steel. Adele cleared her throat. "What do we need to do to get out of here?"

Vanessa didn't trust the way this woman spoke to men with guns. It wasn't placating. There was no fear. She seemed in perfect control. A mask, maybe, but it wasn't a mask that made Vanessa comfortable.

"Inside," the bandaged man said. He took Adele's arm and nudged her in, then did the same to Vanessa.

She jerked her arm away from his sweaty grasp, but he grabbed her again and gave her a shake that had her teeth rattling against each other.

"I ain't afraid to knock you around, tough girl."

Fury razed all the confusion and exhaustion. Knock her around? She'd like to see him try. She struggled to free herself from his meaty grip. "I—"

Dylan's hand rested at the small of her back,

a quiet plea to stop fighting. Even with her heart racing and anger starting to fire through her blood beyond reason and control, the slight pressure of Dylan's big hand reminded her that she wanted to stay alive, no matter how much her temper strained.

She took a deep breath and let her arm go limp against the hand wrapped around it. The goon gave her a good shove inside the cabin, and though she stumbled, she managed to stay upright. She skidded to a stop next to Adele, and noted with more suspicion that Adele didn't even try to stop her skidding slide. Just watched.

Too clinical. Too detached. She was no victim here. Vanessa was almost sure of it.

"Now you, *friend.*" The bandaged man grabbed Dylan by the shirtfront and tossed him inside, hard. Dylan fell gracefully, an easy roll that nearly reminded her of a dancer.

Seriously. Who is this guy?

He was up on his feet in seconds.

"Now, before we get settled, let's get one thing straight. I'm in charge here." The man pointed his gun at Dylan's heart. "You do what I say, or they die." The gun moved to train on Vanessa, but the man's eyes stayed on Dylan. "You're the only one worth anything to me, with your rich daddy."

"You have no idea who you're messing with."

The butt of the weapon hit Dylan's face with

a sickening crack. Vanessa cried out and rushed forward, but the second man shook his head and tsk-tsked, his gun pointed right at her chest.

Dylan got to his feet. "Takes a little more than a pathetic sucker shot to keep me down, you worthless piece of—"

The man raised his weapon again, and Vanessa couldn't just sit back and watch any longer. Heart pounding against her ribs, but with a clarity she hadn't felt since she'd woken up in that van, she jumped forward.

"Wait!"

Everyone looked at her. She didn't know what to say. She'd dealt with violence her whole life, but she'd never been any good at defusing a situation. She was more the stir-it-up type. But things changed. Life changed. She *had* to diffuse this one whether she was any good at it or not.

"We all want to live." She stepped forward again, though she was still behind Dylan. She watched the guns pointed at them warily as she did exactly what he'd done to her.

She lifted her hand and placed it gently if firmly against his back. It was rock hard, like iron. He was tense and ready to fight, but as much as she didn't trust Adele or this situation, she knew two armed men were dangerous. They all had to play this with smarts more than muscle. And she'd had a lifetime of experience doing that.

Though she wouldn't mind finding out a little more about Dylan's impressive muscle.

Where had *that* idiotic thought come from?

"Let's all calm down," she said in a low, controlled voice, far more for Dylan than the bad guys in front of them.

Dylan's chin jutted out, but he flashed a glance at her. Fury. An edgy flash of violence that should have seemed incongruous on Dylan Delaney's perfect face. In this moment, however, it just felt right.

DYLAN WANTED TO pound these two brain-dead barbarians to dust. He could too. They might be bigger, they might have weapons, but he had no doubt he could take them both out. He could even visualize it. A sweep kick here, use one goon's body to slam into the second. A quick gut punch, twist the rifle and use it to knock out the other. Blood. Bones cracking. Victory.

But what he could also visualize in his taking them out was them having an opportunity to hurt Vanessa or Adele. The two women were, very unfortunately, distractions and weaknesses he couldn't afford to ignore.

He let Vanessa's firm pressure on his back be a kind of anchor. He had to think with his brain, not his temper. He even had to be careful not to let his instincts take over.

Because he wasn't surrounded by soldiers. He was surrounded by civilians. Their safety was paramount. Not his.

He turned to face Vanessa, ignoring the men with guns at his back. Her hand fell to her side and she looked at him with a whole slew of emotions in her dark eyes. Not the norm for her. Vanessa usually kept everything locked down.

But there were men with guns, a head injury, amnesia and the fact—whether she believed it or not—she was carrying his baby.

He couldn't lose his temper. He had to be methodical. Like he'd said to her outside, this was the best option right now. Get her taken care of, even if it was by hostage takers, and then he'd find a way for them to escape. No matter what they said or did, he had to be calm. He had to summon all that sniper calm he'd developed and use it here.

He glanced at Adele.

She stood a little behind both of them. He noted she was dressed in jeans and a long-sleeved T-shirt. Not what she would have been wearing at the bank last night. She watched Vanessa with a certain kind of speculation that made the hairs on the back of his neck tingle.

Calculating was the word that came to mind. Not exactly out of character for Adele. She was the calculating sort, but her high opinion of her intelligence often undermined her calculations.

Besides, maybe she was calculating how to get the heck out of the situation, same as he. As much as his instincts warned him something was off with Adele, his brain reasoned it away time and time again.

He was a man who'd spent a chunk of years living by his instincts and pure grit. Had that dulled in these last few years of doing what his father had demanded of him? Had all the fine edges he'd honed inside of himself—so he could live without suffocating in the box his name dictated—softened and been lost?

Now wasn't the time for an identity crisis. He had two women to save and two goons to fight.

He turned to the goons, calm now. Ready to *battle* rather than fight. Fight was instantaneous, with no real endgame. It was anger and revenge. A battle was all about winning. It was about getting these women safe, and making the world— even this tiny corner of it—a righted place.

He would win. Not just for himself, but for this future *child* that would somehow be a part of him. And Vanessa.

Who had to be taken care of at all costs.

"What's the plan, then?" he asked calmly. He'd treat it like a business meeting. They'd discuss what they wanted. He'd discuss what he wanted.

And when he had a good opening, he'd make them wish they'd never been born.

The two men looked at each other, and Dylan didn't have to be a mind reader to understand they weren't the designers of this little plot. They were here for muscle and muscle only.

But who was the boss?

"You two in that room," one said, pointing a gun at a door. "You—" he pointed to Adele "— in that one."

Dylan frowned. It was stupid to split them up. The glossy-looking doors to the rooms weren't at all intimidating, and surely there were windows in the room. He almost asked them if they were sure that's how they wanted to play it, then rolled his eyes at himself.

Adele shuffled off to her room, so Dylan took Vanessa's arm and led her to the other one. He pushed open the door to find what appeared to be an office. There were windows, but they were narrow and lined the very top of the wall. There was no way they could maneuver out of them, even if they could get up there.

One of the men had followed them inside. Dylan eyed him.

"Water. Food. You want me alive, I'll need both," he said, unable to soften the demand into something less abrasive.

"You'll get both. When I'm good and ready."

The man slammed the door, the click of a lock echoing in the room.

It was clearly someone's office. Dylan wondered if they'd be able to figure out who if they snooped enough.

But first things first. He led Vanessa to the most comfortable-looking chair, a rolling, leather desk contraption that at least had some padding. He nudged her into it and, though she went willingly, he saw a flash of the old Vanessa in her expression.

She was still pale with exhaustion, and yet there was a clarity to her eyes that had been missing.

"Your employee is in on this," she said firmly.

Dylan hedged. *In on this* seemed a bit much, and yet... "Something is definitely fishy."

"It's her. All her. When I first stumbled onto her on the road, she didn't act worried or nervous at all. She was very calm and seemed to want me to leave you behind. I didn't know she knew me at first. Then you came and her tune totally changed. *'Oh, we've been worried sick,'*" she mimicked.

Dylan's jaw clenched. "It's off. But..."

"It's *her*," Vanessa insisted.

He nodded. "All right. She's mixed up in it somehow." He could explain away almost everything. Except the change of clothes. If she was as much a victim as they, she'd be in her bank clothes just like he was.

He shrugged out of the now-tattered suit jacket and laid it across Vanessa's lap. "You need water, food and rest." What she really needed was a doctor. He'd find a way. He *would*. "We should look around. See if we can figure out who owns this place."

She looked up at the windows, and he could see her come to the same conclusion he had. There was no getting out that way. "We have to get out of here."

"We will. My father will pay—"

"The ransom business is crap. You know it and I know it. There's more to this than money, and even if Daddy Big Bucks would pay, I don't think Laurel and her precious police department would feel the same."

"I think the people we love would do anything to keep us safe."

"Keep *you* safe, goose."

Dylan wanted to laugh, but there was something vulnerable in the words no matter how sharply she said them. He crouched in front of her, took her hands in his and squeezed. He noted the surprise and suspicion in her eyes, and ignored both.

"No matter what you remember or don't, you know your brother would move heaven and earth to keep you safe. If he knows you're missing, he's out there looking for you. Noah and Ty too."

"They'd have to know I was missing."

"They will. Soon enough."

Chapter Seven

Back in Bent, Vanessa's mechanic shop

"She wouldn't."

Laurel looked at the firm, furious line of her husband's mouth and rubbed at the headache pounding at her temples. As much as she agreed with Grady's estimation of Vanessa not leaving town on her own, his lack of cooperation was grating on her nerves.

Grady had let them into Vanessa's place to look around, and while there weren't any cut-and-dried clues, her motorcycle was missing. Everything else was where it should be. Hart's supposition that Vanessa had left of her own accord on said motorcycle had not gone over well with Laurel's husband.

"Hart isn't asking if she *did* skip town, since we don't know," Laurel said, keeping her voice calm and no-nonsense. "We're asking what you think it would take for Vanessa to leave without telling anyone."

"It wouldn't take anything, because Vanessa wouldn't take off without a word to anyone no matter what was up." He lifted the bill from an ob-gyn's office in Fremont they'd found when searching her above-the-shop apartment. "Pregnancy wouldn't be a reason. She knows we'd support her. No matter what. She wouldn't be *scared* or running from anything."

Laurel had to keep her mouth shut. Since she'd been dealing with her own, there'd been a few times in the past few weeks she'd looked at Vanessa and wondered. Yet Vanessa had been with no man, and showed no signs of telling her family about her condition. So, *obviously*, it wasn't totally clear-cut knowing she'd be supported.

But Grady continued to thunder his irritation. Luckily, Laurel knew enough about her husband to understand that was bluster covering up his fear. She couldn't afford to be soft, but it was hard when she was worried too.

"She sure as hell wouldn't have disappeared on her *motorcycle* and left her car at the Delaney Bank of all places," Grady continued furiously.

"Easy highway access," Hart countered, impressing Laurel with how even and calm he was being in the face of Grady's notable temper. "Kind of hidden. If she didn't want to be—"

Grady growled and Laurel pressed a hand to his chest. He was angry, but that anger hid a deep worry and fear. She felt it too. It had been a long time since she and Vanessa had been friends. Even marrying Grady hadn't smoothed things over from their teenage years, though it had softened some of the edge.

The Vanessa she knew—thought she knew anyway—wouldn't run away from anything. And if Laurel thought about *Vanessa*, she didn't have to think about the fact her brother was missing too. Without thinking the move through she pressed a hand to her stomach.

She heard Grady's sigh as his arm came around her shoulders. Despite her uniform, and the fact she was here in an official capacity, he pressed a kiss to her temple.

"What can we *do*?" he asked.

It helped ease a tiny fraction of tension in Laurel that he asked it of Hart, and helped her anxiety even more when Hart answered, plainly and certainly.

"You trust me to investigate." He smiled a little sheepishly. "And Laurel, of course. If you find any hints of what might be going on with Vanessa, you tell the police. Give the same instructions to any and all family members. Work with us. We want everyone home and safe, same as you."

Laurel's phone trilled. She would have ignored it, but the Delaney Ranch's number gave her stomach a little jolt. She answered, stepping away from Grady's arm.

"Laurel?"

She frowned at the grave tone in her father's greeting. "What is it?"

"I was catching up on my email," Dad began. "I hadn't had a chance to check since I'd been driving home from the airport, then I was distracted last night, obviously. I have one from Dylan dated yesterday that says he'll be gone for a while. No explanation. Just that he had to leave town."

"Forward it," Laurel said automatically, ending the call to wait for the email.

"Dad has an email from Dylan dated yesterday saying he'd be out of town for a while. He's forwarding it to me."

"Maybe they ran off together," Hart said, gesturing to Vanessa's place.

Grady snorted. "Sure. I mean, maybe to murder each other. But definitely not *together*."

"Erm…"

Laurel stared at Hart, noticing the odd flush to his cheeks. "Erm *what*?" she demanded.

"Well, it's just…" He cleared his throat. "They didn't exactly look murderous at your wedding reception. Quite the opposite."

Both Grady and Laurel stared at Hart with matching dumbfounded expressions.

"You know, I left early because I had the early shift the next morning, and I happened to see them leave together."

Laurel rolled her eyes. "Maybe they left at the same time, but not *together*. They were probably arguing on their way out."

"Oh, no. They were very much together and very much not arguing. Hard to argue when you've got your tongues down each other's throats. I gave them a ride back to Vanessa's because they were far too drunk to drive." Hart nodded at the medical bill Grady had tossed back onto the desk earlier.

"No." Laurel and Grady gasped in unison.

Her upstanding, somewhat-inflexible brother would never... He'd never... She glanced at Grady. There'd been a time *she'd* have never, but she'd never cared about the feud the way Dylan did.

"Seriously though, they were drunk as skunks," Hart continued. "Believe you me. Definitely on the road to a bad decision. Maybe even one with consequences. Could be they ran off together to deal with them."

Laurel looked up at Grady. It made a strange kind of sense, even though she couldn't truly believe it. Vanessa and Dylan. It had to be impossible.

"Impossible," Grady confirmed, as if reading her thoughts.

Her phone's incoming-email sound dinged and Laurel shook her head. She had to focus on fact, not supposition.

She pulled up the forwarded email and read the words with a frown.

Be gone for a bit. Don't worry. Explain when I get back. Adele can cover at the bank for me. —Dylan

She showed Hart, then Grady.

"Except Adele is missing too," Hart pointed out.

"Nothing adds up," Laurel said, staring at the email. While she could see Vanessa skipping town on her motorcycle, she couldn't see her doing it without tying up loose ends at her shop. And Dylan would never leave the bank so abruptly—especially unlocked.

But she felt a niggle of concern over the possibility Dylan and Vanessa had hooked up drunkenly at her wedding, conceived a child and were now both missing. They'd be embarrassed. Probably horrified. Enough to skip town?

But Adele Oscar was the thing that threw a wrench into all this. Laurel and Hart had been by her house last night and this morning. She hadn't been home. Everything had been locked and secure, and her car hadn't been seen, though they'd put out an APB.

"We need to find Adele Oscar," Hart said. "Search warrant for her house?"

Laurel nodded. Adele was the key.

Chapter Eight

A little while later, after watching Dylan meticulously search through everything in the room, then stalk around it, reminding her of a wolf—or some other dangerous predator—the door swung open.

The man she'd come to think of as Eyeballs, because his were the size of saucers, tossed a paper plate onto the desk. Then threw a bottle of water at Dylan. Hard.

Dylan caught it without a flinch, which made Eyeballs scowl. Without a word, Eyeballs closed the door and locked it again.

The heavy, almost chemical smell of the microwave pizza pocket made Vanessa dry heave, but she didn't throw up. That was a plus.

Dylan watched her with both concern and a kind of detached study. "You have to eat it," he said after a few seconds.

"Eating it won't help if I just throw it all up."

"You don't know that. Plus, vomit might be an excellent diversion."

She laughed against her will, but it died quickly when he crouched in front of her again, holding the plate with the offensive microwave meal in one hand. He held out the water bottle with the other.

"This atrocity is still frozen in the middle, but I'm going to break off a small piece of the cooked edge. Eat. Drink. That should help keep it down."

"I don't need you to feed me." But she took the water, even as she eyed his movements warily.

He watched her with those steady brown eyes. Something in her chest fluttered—a light, airy feeling directly in contrast with their situation. With how she'd always felt about Dylan.

He disgusted her. He made her sneer. He made her *hate*. She had never had one positive feeling toward Dylan or one positive interaction with him.

But in the past twenty-four hours, he'd displayed a warmth she'd never seen and a resourceful strength she never would have believed. The man had fought off two armed men, and if not for her, and perhaps Adele, she had no doubt he'd be back in Bent, having happily dispatched all the bad guys.

Maybe it was just the beard that made her feel differently toward him. She was a sucker for beards, and his scruff was growing in fast and full and handsome.

She'd rather blame facial hair than her previous conclusions about him being wrong.

He broke off a piece of the gummy crust and held it up to her lips. Their eyes met, held. Something shuddered through her. She wanted to believe it was doom, gloom and hell, but it was lighter, sweeter, and some foreign part of her wanted to lean into it.

She could see him, clean-shaven and harsh-looking, in the dim light of another room. A flash of something. Hands on her face. He wasn't touching her, but she could feel him. She could remember the register of shock at—

"You have a tattoo."

He raised an eyebrow, slipped the food into her mouth. She chewed and swallowed, so distracted by that odd flash of memory her stomach didn't even turn.

"Do I?"

"I couldn't make it out. It was dark. But you were shirtless. And you had a tattoo." It wasn't the first little burst of memory she'd had, but it was the clearest. And the most nonsensical. "Fill in the blanks for me."

He pulled off another piece of the crust, held it up to her mouth. "I don't know your blanks, Vanessa."

"Then fill in yours."

She could sense he didn't want to, but she could

also tell he had taken responsibility for this mess. He thought it was his fault. He felt beholden to her.

She wasn't about to ignore the fact she could *use* that. She refused to take the bite and he sighed.

"Fine. You eat this, and I'll tell you as much as I can."

She nodded, letting him feed her small bites as she sipped water in between them. She realized he was picking off the heated pieces, and when he just had the frozen center left, he ate that himself.

It shouldn't surprise her he was noble. He *was* a Delaney, after all. Maybe the most condescending, high-horsed, snobbish Delaney of the bunch—next to his father—but noble tendencies ran in that clan.

What surprised her was that she was *moved* by the display of caretaking. She'd never wanted someone to take care of her. That made you beholden to them, and she would never let that happen to her. A Carson had to get by on their own wits. Sure, when she got in trouble Grady, Noah or Ty had stepped in and defended her. But no one had ever fed her and taken the crap ends for themselves.

That you remember.

"I have a tattoo," he said after his last swallow. "The only place you would have seen it is during our..."

She couldn't help the curve of her mouth. "Afraid to say the words, sweetheart?"

"See? You needed to eat. You're practically back to normal."

Except she didn't remember. Not really. Not in the way she needed to. She breathed through the panic that she might have lost thirteen years she'd never retrieve. At least she was alive to have more years.

"We had sex. I know that because I woke up naked next to you, also naked, the morning after Laurel and Grady's wedding. I don't—"

"Laurel and *Grady*?" she all but screeched.

He pressed his lips together, but his mouth curved anyway. "Don't worry. You made your outrage well known in the moment."

"My brother married... He couldn't have... *Married?*"

"Happily, even. Much as I'd like to deny it."

"But Laurel is such a do-gooder. She...she's a cop, isn't she?" Vanessa pressed fingers to her aching head. The food had helped her feel less shaky, but her brain hurt. "She always wanted to be. She'd have done it. She did. She helped..." But whatever fuzzy memory she'd been bringing to life faded. She swore.

"Easy," Dylan said quietly. "You're remember-

ing bits and pieces. That makes me think it'll all
come back, but we have some more important
things at hand."

Vanessa scowled at the door. "Yes, we do. But
tell me what happened. How we got here."

He recounted her coming to see him, the shooting from the front of the bank and their treach-
erous ride in the van. Vanessa didn't remember
any of it, but she thought of Adele.

"She changed her clothes."

When she met Dylan's gaze, she knew he'd already put that together.

"And they separated us," Vanessa continued,
working through all her suspicions, "because
she's involved. If they had any sense at all, they'd
put you alone since you're the money shot."

He winced at the term, which would have made
her laugh if she wasn't so angry at Adele and her
little farce.

"I bet a hundred bucks this is her place."

His mouth quirked. "A bet is what got you into
this mess."

She racked her memory, but couldn't come up
with it. So she focused on the here and now. "She
works at the bank. For you and your father. She'd
know your schedule." They had to figure out how
Adele was connected, and if they did, maybe this
would make more sense. Maybe they could find
a way out.

"I would have been gone if not for you though."

"But you weren't gone. Your car was still there, right?"

"Right. But, she's worked for us for years. I can't believe—"

"What do you know about her?"

"She started as a teller. Moved from… I want to say Denver. Maybe Seattle. Some big city. She'd worked at a bank there and wanted the small-town life. Dad liked the idea of an outsider."

"That doesn't sound like your father."

"Better an outsider than a Carson or Carson sympathizer."

"Now, *that* sounds just like him."

"She had a kind of polish. She was a hard worker and moved up the ranks quickly. By the time I…came back home from college, she was second only to the assistant manager. A position Dad held for me."

"Came back. College. You say that so weird."

"Do I?"

"And you use that haughty tone to say 'do I' whenever something gets too close. Came back with your fancy finance degree."

"That's what they say."

Why was he talking in riddles about something so insignificant? It didn't make any sense. "What do *you* say?"

He shrugged. "Doesn't matter."

"Maybe it matters to me."

His eyes met hers, that same odd fluttering stirring in her breast, a little too close to her heart. But she didn't break his gaze, and she didn't back away. Maybe she'd lost her sense as well as her memory, but she couldn't bring herself to care.

POWER. THEY'D ALWAYS created powerful reactions in each other. Once hate. Now...the thing that crackled between them had altered. He wanted to touch her. His memories of that night were misty, probably like her memory of the past thirteen years, and yet he had images, odd feelings, like he could remember a rightness when their bodies joined.

He broke her gaze. He didn't believe in rightness or feelings. Reason mattered. Facts mattered.

Yet he was a man who'd shrugged off both and lived a lie for years, all so he could stand to live a different lie.

He stood, taking a few steps away from where he'd deposited her on that chair however long ago. It wasn't so much a retreat as a recentering. "We need to focus on—"

"No, don't brush me off. You're at the center of this. They weren't after me. I was a hapless bystander because we got drunk and stupid, apparently, if I believe that."

He raised an eyebrow and she huffed out a breath. "Okay, *fine.* I believe we drunkenly hooked up, and I really hope I'm pregnant because I feel too much like crap to not have a reason. But, regardless, you're the center. Those men supposedly want a ransom for *you.*"

"Supposedly." It didn't add up so clearly though, since he would have left the bank if Vanessa hadn't come. Since he didn't have a set schedule in the office that someone could have gleaned information from. Since it didn't seem like they'd taken any money from the bank—if money was what they were after.

Whoever those men were, whatever their purpose, it did have to do with him.

It would have been easy enough to see his car in the lot and act. But Adele had been there too.

Only one. But the men had three.

Adele had changed her clothes. He couldn't get past that one simple fact. He was still in his suit—dirty and tattered as it might be. Vanessa still had on the outfit she'd come to see him in. Yet Adele had changed into jeans and a clean shirt. And she didn't seem scared.

"If she's involved, the bank is involved."

"Which means money is involved," Vanessa supplied.

"I suppose."

"Did she have money troubles?"

"I don't know anything about Adele's personal life. Even if she didn't keep to herself, she's…"

"She's what?"

"It's hard to explain. She's perfectly nice, but underneath that is an abrasiveness. I wouldn't say anyone really *likes* Adele. Truth is, no matter how she tries to hide it—and I think she does try—she thinks she's smarter than everyone, a harder worker. She thinks she's better."

Vanessa snorted. "She must fit right in with the Delaneys."

He shot her a bland look. "But there's no tension. No fights. She's never been demoted or scolded. She'd have no reason to hate me or the bank as an entity."

"What about your father? Would she have a reason to hate him?"

"I want to say it's the same, but…"

"But what?"

He rubbed the back of his neck. He didn't like parading his father's faults in front of anyone, let alone a Carson. "He isn't quite the stand-up guy I'd always assumed him to be." Dylan thought regretfully of what they'd found out last year about his father's extracurricular activities: an affair with a married woman. A *Carson* woman. It wasn't exactly murder or anything, but it had shaken Dylan's foundation of believing his father a good, if hard, man.

"So she could have had an issue with your father?"

"I suppose. But why not go after him?"

Vanessa rolled her eyes. "Don't you watch any movies? You don't go after the person you hate. You go after what they love."

It made sense. Uncomfortable sense, but sense nonetheless. "If that's the case—if this is some sort of revenge against my father—then I don't think she plans on me surviving. Get a ransom, kill me off?" He didn't shudder, didn't worry, because he'd like to see someone try to get rid of him. *Everyone* underestimated him. Even Adele.

Even Vanessa.

Vanessa watched him, consideration all over her face. "They made a big production about keeping you alive. Maybe it's to give weight to the ransom story, or maybe she's got something against you too."

"What would she have against me?"

"Same thing the rest of us peons do, Dylan. You're a jerk."

He puffed up, insulted even though he couldn't figure out why Vanessa's normal estimation of him would be insulting.

"Just like I'm a jerk. People hate us because we don't play nice. I say it like it is, and you ice out the world. Maybe it's not who we are underneath, but it's what people see."

"So what are you underneath, Vanessa Carson?" He hadn't meant that to come out sounding sexual, but it had. His body warmed, tightened. Because even if he couldn't remember the details of the act, there was a feeling he got when he thought about them being together. It was very nearly irresistible.

Nearly.

Chapter Nine

Heat flooded through Vanessa, and worse, a beat of arousal she couldn't deny no matter how much she wanted to. Her skin prickled and her core hummed with need.

Jeez.

She tried to swallow through her dry throat. Then, realizing she still held the water bottle from before, unscrewed the cap and took an unsteady breath. She could not have sexual thoughts about Dylan, period, but most especially when they were abducted by goons. And yet there those sexual thoughts were.

"We should focus on you," she managed, hoping she sounded stabler than she felt. "I'm an incidental."

He made a noise, one she didn't know how to characterize, though she thought it had to do with guilt. But he didn't press. Which meant *she* had to press her one advantage.

"And since I'm here because of you, we need to

figure this out. Which means focusing on Adele. And you."

"Yeah. I suppose it's possible she wanted my position."

"Wouldn't anyone? I mean anyone who worked in that bank. Certainly not *anyone*." She'd rather jump out a window than try her hand at staid, businessy bankerland.

"Everyone knew that position was mine. He held it for me while I was…away."

"You're going to have to explain that." Why he got so fidgety every time his years at college were mentioned.

But he ignored her. "It'd have been pointless and stupid to think she or anyone else would get that position. I don't think Adele is stupid."

"No, but people are oftentimes foolish even if you don't think they should be." *We slept together.* It seemed the height of pointless and stupid.

"Stupid enough to kidnap? To send armed men after me? I can't believe it, Vanessa. I really can't. She might be a hard lady, but she isn't a psychopath."

Vanessa thought of her father and her uncle. No one had considered them *psychopaths*. Jerks, sure. Alcoholics, maybe. But the fact they liked to use their fists on women went mostly ignored, no matter how incomprehensible that act was to a normal person.

Noah and Ty had considered their father a monster when he'd been alive. Grady didn't know much about what their father had done in his absence.

She sighed. Old wounds had no place here. *She* had no place here, and yet here she was.

She felt a little bit better, a little bit steadier, now that she'd had water and food. Her brain didn't feel so foggy and her body didn't feel as though the wrong move would send everything inside of her rushing out.

"It has to relate to the bank," she continued, trying to muse through the problem aloud. "Maybe not you. Maybe your father."

Dylan's eyebrows drew together. "But I'm here."

"Sure. You're daddy's pride and joy though. So it could be you. It could be him. It could be about both of you. Delaneys in general."

"You'd like that, wouldn't you?"

"Probably under any other circumstances, but not when I'm tied to you and in this mess. But you said we were abducted at the bank. Adele is somehow weirdly mixed up in this. It has to connect to the bank."

"They said they wanted a ransom," Dylan said, taking her threads and adding some of his own thoughts to it. "Maybe it *is* just a ploy to get a bunch of money from my father." He shook his head. "Doesn't sit right though. There'd be easier, smarter ways to do that."

"Maybe. Maybe not. Adele wants money, needs money maybe? She pretends she's a victim and no one ever knows she has anything to do with it. She gets off scot-free. Biggest problem is I got in the way."

Dylan seemed to consider, *really* consider her words. She hadn't expected him to. She was used to dismissal from a Delaney, especially *him*.

"If it's about the money, I feel like there were better ways to get it than kidnapping. Adele has access to all sorts of things at the bank. She could have embezzled, stolen, cheated. Carefully."

"But not easily."

"I hear kidnapping is so easy."

Vanessa ignored his dry comment. "Everything she could have done at the bank would have been traced to her."

Dylan's mouth quirked, causing that weird, annoying, unwelcome feeling to flutter in her chest again.

"You've got a sharp mind, Vanessa."

"Imagine that," she returned dryly.

"Considered robbing a few banks now and again?"

She wanted to be offended, but mostly the

tongue-in-cheek way he said it made her want to laugh. *With* him rather than *at* him. "Oh, I've considered all *sorts* of things, Delaney."

That flash of a grin had unwanted lust pooling low in her belly. She'd always thought he was attractive. She'd just hated everything about him underneath the physical. Now everything was getting muddled.

Head injury. She'd blame the head injury. And change the subject. "You fail out of college or something?"

"Huh?"

"You're squirrelly every time it comes up. Something happened while you were away. I want to know what. Maybe it connects."

"It doesn't."

"Maybe it does."

"It doesn't."

She huffed out an annoyed breath.

"I didn't fail. I—"

The door burst open. The goon she'd decided to call No-Neck stood there, holding that gun like it was some proof of his epic power. Vanessa wanted to sneer, but she held back the nasty look at the last second.

Now that she was feeling more herself, it was going to be quite the fight not to be *too* much herself and piss off the men with guns.

"You." He pointed the gun at Dylan. "Out front."

Vanessa jumped to her feet, even as Dylan began to move to go with the man. "You can't separate us."

No-Neck laughed. "I can do whatever I want, little girl."

Dylan gave her a sharp look. "Stay here. Stay put." He gave a pointed look at her stomach.

She brought a hand to it without thinking. For the first time, she really, truly believed him without reservation. She was pregnant with his baby, and he'd protect her—and it—at all costs.

The knowledge, the acceptance, shook her to hell and back.

DYLAN FOLLOWED THE muscle-bound idiot into the living room, noting everything he saw. There was a phone on the table next to the couch. He filed it away. Furniture, art on the walls, windows. He took note which way the sun slanted outside the blinds when he could tell.

When he got them out of this mess, he'd know how to lead police or anyone else to this place and make sure these men—and their boss—paid for what they'd done. That was a promise he'd make to himself, and he was not in a habit of breaking those.

The gun-toting moron shoved him onto a plush leather couch. Expensive, Dylan noted. Whoever owned this cabin had money, which meant they weren't likely *after* money.

He filed that away too.

"You're going to make a phone call. One of those FaceTime deals."

Dylan tried not to let his excitement show. Were they *stupid*? Even if they didn't let him say anything of importance, a FaceTime call would show a background. It would give Dad some hints, some ideas. A damn *lead* to hand over to Laurel and the police.

He fixed a disgusted look on his face and put as much sarcasm into his voice as he could manage. "Lucky me."

The man raised the butt of his weapon and Dylan forced his body to relax so when he took the blow it didn't meet resistance. It'd hurt like hell, he knew, considering his face was already throbbing from all the blows, but it'd help downplay whatever injury he got in the long run.

But the second guy came out of what Dylan supposed was some kind of kitchen area off to the side of the living room. "Remember what Boss said."

The guy with the gun grunted, lowered the weapon with a lot of regret. Dylan smirked.

Which earned him a meaty fist to the gut. Dylan wheezed out a painful breath, doubling over and seeing stars.

The goon in the kitchen sighed.

The one who'd punched him laughed. "Boss said no more messing with his face. That wasn't his face."

"Your funeral," the other one said.

Dylan sure as hell hoped so.

Slowly, he sat back up. Even though just about everything on his body hurt at this point, he wouldn't let anyone see it. Goons or Vanessa or…

"Where's Adele?"

"She's in her room, just like you two were in yours. She gets the nicer digs because she cooperated."

"She wasn't in the van with us."

"So?"

"Changed her clothes too."

The guy in front of him flashed a look to the guy in the kitchen area. Dylan tried not to react, but that hesitation, that look, told him a lot. Because they hadn't expected him to question Adele's place in all this.

Then the man in front of him threw his head back and laughed. "Yeah, sure. The blonde's the real mastermind behind this whole thing. You figured us out. Maybe I'll go turn myself in now, since I got this sharp detective on my heels."

The other man laughed too. Uproariously.

Dylan didn't buy it. It might have planted a seed or two of doubt but barely. Still, he let that doubt show. He wasn't going to take the smarter-than-you tactic or the dumber-than-a-box-of-rocks one either. He had to mix it up. Keep them off-balance.

"Go get the blonde to unlock her phone," living-room guy ordered of kitchen guy. "She's got the old man's number on her phone."

Even though Adele would of course have his father's number in her phone, Dylan thought it was an odd request. FaceTime. Adele's phone. There was a convenience to their plan Dylan didn't trust.

Or was it smart? Use her phone, then there'd be no way to trace it to anyone besides Adele. Adele had access to his father, and having that kind of insurance was smart if they thought he was going to be uncooperative.

Maybe this *was* simply about money, and Adele was unconnected.

But she had changed clothes, hadn't been hurt in the initial break-in, and the men had distinctly said they were only supposed to kidnap one person.

Either way, if someone knew Adele was missing and they used her phone, it could be pinged. It might take some time—Dylan knew from Laurel there were all sorts of legalities to jump through before the police could access that information—but it was a chance.

The second man brought Adele out. She still looked put together, but her eyes were a little wide. Dylan almost believed she was scared.

Almost.

"C-can't I just tell you the c-code?" she stuttered, as the man with the gun held it out to her. Her fingers fumbled with it and it fell to the floor.

One of the goons nudged it with his foot. "Pick it up and fix it up for us," he ordered, gesturing toward a little tripod they'd set up. "Get him in the shot, then make the call."

"You could just record a video and send it," Dylan suggested. He doubted they'd take the hook, but it was worth a shot. A video could be watched, studied. A FaceTime call... Dad would have to know how to take a screenshot and have the presence of mind to do so.

The man shook his head. "Boss's orders are clear, friend."

Adele was shaking as she set up the phone on the tripod. Convincing nerves, and yet Dylan didn't *feel* convinced.

Still, regardless of her innocence or guilt, she had a phone. That phone was the best shot he had, as long as people knew they were missing.

Surely Laurel knew at this point they were all missing in a capacity that required police involvement. *Surely.* His sister was a good cop and a damn smart detective. He had to trust she was on this.

"Th-there. I think it's all set up. I just have to click the movie icon."

"Sit next to him. Don't speak."

Adele nodded and took a seat next to Dylan on the couch. She seemed to vibrate, and his first thought was nerves, but there was a look in her eye, a lack of tension in her expression. He wanted to believe she was scared and that she was being forced to do this.

But Dylan couldn't shake all the strange little pieces of this mystery.

One of the men shoved a piece of paper at him.

"You'll say that, and nothing else, or things won't end well for your friend in there." He pointed his gun toward the room Vanessa was in. "Read when I say go. Even if he talks over you, you read it once and then I disconnect."

Dylan looked down at the paper. The statement was simple: I'm in grave danger. Instructions on how to deliver money. No mention of Vanessa. Or Adele, even though she was clearly going to be in the shot.

Dylan looked up at the man, then the phone. He didn't allow himself a glance at the door where Vanessa was. Didn't allow himself to think about the fact they might hurt her. He had to focus on any possible way to figure out what was really going on here.

If he knew the facts, the players, he could get everyone out with minimum fuss. He believed that.

"All right, friend. The minute Daddy Money Bags answers, you read."

Dylan nodded. He could still feel the vibrations coming off Adele next to him, and yet he forced himself to focus on his core. The deep steadiness within his soul. He'd learned to compartmentalize as a soldier. Learned to live within the mission and nothing else as a sniper.

When his dad answered, the small rectangle of his face showing concern and fear and hope before he even managed a word, Dylan felt nothing.

He looked down and began to read.

Chapter Ten

Back in Bent, at the Delaney Ranch

Laurel had her father go through it again. And again. She had him write down everything he remembered, and she wrote it down as he recounted his version of the phone call, as well.

She was worried for her brother, even for poor Adele, who seemed to be an innocent bystander now. Laurel believed she could save them though—had to believe it.

What made her sick to her stomach was that there was no mention or glimpse of Vanessa. She was going to have to go home to her husband and tell him that his sister may have run off without a word.

He wouldn't believe her.

She didn't believe her.

Vanessa's car in the bank parking lot was too much. If it had been found *anywhere* else, she'd feel the same as Hart—convinced Vanessa had run off to go have her baby far away from her family.

But even if Dylan was the father of Vanessa's baby—a theory Laurel had an even harder time believing—there was no reason, excuse or sensible explanation for Vanessa's car being in the Delaney Bank parking lot.

"It was new," Dad said, relaying that detail for the fourth or fifth time. He sat at the Delaney kitchen table, looking pale and shaky and as disheveled as Laurel had ever seen him. He hadn't even been this upset when her mother had died or when he'd been mixed up in a threat to his life by Jesse Carson last year.

"I could tell the cabin around him was new. You could look at new cabins. Surely builders have records and…"

She tried to smile reassuringly at her father. "Hart's already on that from your first statement. We'll have the names of anyone who's built or bought a cabin in the county within the last year. It's a good place to start. And now we're trying to ping Adele's phone. We've got clues. Hard leads."

Dad looked at her imploringly. Apparently seeing Dylan on that video had eradicated his usual control. He was worried sick. It poked at Laurel's own sense of calm, but she was a cop. She had to be a cop now more than ever.

"What if they're not in the county?" Dad asked. "Or even the *state*?"

His words spoke to her own fears, but she couldn't show that to her father. "It's unlikely." A lie, but it was for the best for now.

Dad pushed back from the table and started pacing. "I need to send the money."

"You don't have the money. Besides, they'll only escalate and ask for more. You have to—"

He whirled. "I have the bank. I have access to all the money we need."

"Dad, you can't... That isn't legal. You know it and I know it."

"I could sell the cattle and pay it all back. I could sell everything if I had to. I could—"

"You could, but right now you have to sit down." She took a breath and brought him back to his chair. She had to steady herself. If he'd been cold or demanding, it would have been easy. But Dad shaking, falling apart like this, made tears burn in the back of her eyes.

She wouldn't cry. She was a Delaney. Police officer. *Sister.* She swallowed at the lump in her throat. She could only be one thing here. The law. "You need to calm down, and let me and the rest of the police do our job."

"Laurel, your brother—"

Her heart cracked, but she didn't let it show. "I know. Trust me, I know. But we've called state, and they've got to look into this before I can let you pay off that ransom. It's rare a kidnapper gets the money and lets the abductee go. This whole thing is rare, but let's give state time to get caught up to speed."

"We should call the FBI."

"If there's a need, we will. State will. I can only do so much with my resources at county. But I'm doing everything I can."

Dad looked at her, and some of that cold disdain she'd grown used to since falling for Grady was back in his expression.

"Are you?" he asked coolly.

It hurt, even if she convinced herself it was his fear and temper talking.

She pressed her fingers to the table, taking a moment to steady herself when an unwanted wave of dizziness settled over her. She needed to eat. *Baby* needed to eat.

She glanced at her father, who still didn't know. And wouldn't approve. Bad enough to marry a Carson, but to procreate with one?

She almost smiled. If it was true Vanessa was pregnant with Dylan's baby, she'd get them home just to see the look on her father's face.

"Dylan is smart and resourceful. I don't know Adele that well, but she strikes me as someone who can keep her head in the midst of a crisis. I trust Hart to help me on this investigation, and I trust state to make the right call on when, if and how we should pay the ransom. You don't have to trust those things, Dad. You don't have to trust me. But it'd be a lot better for you, and Dylan, if you did."

"I'll never forgive you if anything happens to him," Dad said, cold and decisive. Yes, this was the father she'd known for the past year.

"Don't worry. I won't forgive myself either."

"You brought this on us. You've *cursed* us."

Her father's hatred of the Carsons had never shocked her, but this did. To the core. "Dad, you don't believe that."

"I absolutely believe this town has been in turmoil since you dared let that stain touch you. How many times has a Delaney been hurt since you—"

"I won't listen to this." She whirled away. It was too much. Too much blame when she was struggling with her own. "You'll sit tight," she ordered, striding away from him even as she barked out each word. "I've warned Jen to keep an eye on you. Don't make me bring in Cam." But she'd call her other brother nevertheless to make sure he kept an eye on the finances. If her father compounded this mess with a crime…

She couldn't think of it. She had a case to solve.

Dad said nothing else, and she let herself out. She stopped on the porch and took a deep breath of Wyoming air. The ranch was still, the quiet only interrupted by the breeze or an occasional cow lowing in the distance.

It was home, or had been. Now her home was with Grady and this baby of theirs. The world was changing. Bent was changing.

Curses. She didn't believe in curses. She'd never believed in the Carson-Delaney feud that had kept two families sniping at each other for over a century. She wouldn't start now, and she'd never, ever allow anything to make her believe there was a curse when Grady was everything she'd ever needed.

But no matter how many certain, powerful words she told herself in her head, a flutter of fear beat against her gut.

Chapter Eleven

Not having a clock was sending Vanessa into a low-level panic attack. How long had Dylan been out there? How long would she be in here alone?

She'd never had trouble being alone before. In fact, it was her preferred state of being. At least, when she was in charge of her own life. Turned out, kidnapping was wreaking havoc with her sense of the usual.

Plus, she'd drunk the entire bottle of water. Which meant she really, really needed to get out of here.

But something held her back. No, not something. She knew exactly what held her back. It was just hard to admit.

Fear. She was petrified of what existed outside those doors. What if they'd killed Dylan? Tortured him? He might be some kind of secret tough guy, but two men with guns were with him out there.

Ransom. They were after a ransom. They wouldn't kill their star in the ransom show.

Except they were morons. And whoever was the boss—and in Vanessa's mind that was Adele—had this cabin, which had to have cost a pretty penny. It wasn't about money.

Unless it was. Money could dry up. A person could always need more.

Where was Dylan?

Vanessa squeezed her eyes shut. She wasn't a coward, and since she was feeling mostly normal, she couldn't even blame it on a head injury or this…pregnancy thing. She couldn't be a coward. It wasn't allowed.

She moved forward to the door and started banging on it. She didn't stop until it opened—though just a crack.

"Knock it off," No-Neck growled, his beady little eye visible through the crack.

"I have to go to the bathroom."

There were murmurs, grumbles, then after a few minutes of shuffling, the door opened the rest of the way.

One big hand gripped her upper arm and gave her a jerk, and then he had her other arm in his grasp so that both arms were pulled behind her back and he could guide her.

She immediately searched the living area for Dylan, though it only took a second for her eyes to be drawn to the figure on the couch. He sat, ramrod straight, in the middle of it. They'd tied his hands and his feet, and she got the impression—though she couldn't see it—that something was making him have that absurdly straight posture.

Then there was the strip of duct tape across his mouth. He didn't look at her, kept his gaze straight ahead, which again she wondered if it had to do with how they'd tied him up.

But through it all, even as the goon pushed her to a bathroom, Dylan looked…bored. No fear. No worry. Just like he couldn't believe he was letting himself be subjected to this.

Such a Delaney. For the first time in her entire life, that made her smile. And the smile made her maybe a little too brave.

"Where's your chick boss?" Vanessa asked of the jerk holding her arms.

The man didn't answer. He just shoved her forward by his grasp on her arms. Vanessa supposed he was leading her to the bathroom. As she passed Dylan, he inclined his head slightly to the other room, still not making eye contact. Apparently, Adele was still in there.

The man pushed her through a door, and she stumbled forward, catching herself on the sink when he let her go. She glared at him. He smiled his smarmy smile. "Three minutes. Time starts now." And he shut the door.

Irritated and furious, Vanessa quickly did what her body demanded. Washing her hands, she looked at herself in the mirror. Her hair was a tangled mess. She was pale and dirty. There were shadows under her eyes.

"One minute left," the man outside called.

Indulging herself, she stuck her tongue out at the door before letting her gaze sweep the small half bath she was in.

Another narrow line of windows she couldn't possibly slither out of, high on the walls. She crouched and opened the cabinet underneath the sink, pushed through rolls of toilet paper and hand towels, searching for anything that could be a weapon or a clue.

Nothing.

"Time's up!"

Vanessa straightened just as the door swung open. He didn't immediately grab her. Instead, he watched her, leaning against the doorjamb.

"You're lucky, you know."

She rolled her eyes. "Yeah, I'm a regular fairy princess."

"If I was in charge?" He let his gaze take a tour of her body that had her stomach roiling. "Things would be *very* different for you, *fairy princess*."

She wanted to tell him things would be very

different because she would have cut off his balls, but she bit her tongue and held his disgusting stare with a bland one of her own.

"Who hired you two apes? You don't have one brain between you," Dylan called out.

Her own eyes widened, even as No-Neck's did. How was Dylan talking? He'd just had tape on his mouth and...

"How the hell'd he get out of the tape?" the man grumbled, turning his back on Vanessa.

Vanessa had a flash of attacking No-Neck. Just jumping on his back and going at it. He might be stronger, but she was strong herself. Wiry and quick. She knew how to punch a guy's lights out with the element of surprise.

But he had a gun, and she was apparently growing a baby.

Then the moment was over. No-Neck remembered himself, grabbed her by the arm and jerked her out into the living room.

Eyeballs was standing over Dylan, fury and something like bafflement written in every ugly line of his expression.

"How'd you get it off?" he demanded, nudging Dylan's side with the gun he never seemed to put down.

Dylan smiled up at him. "Magic."

The butt of Eyeballs's weapon struck Dylan's stomach. Hard. Dylan bent over, even gasped out a breath, but when he straightened into a sitting position on the couch again, his expression didn't radiate pain or fury. He was just grinning.

Maybe *he* was a psychopath.

"How'd you get it off?" Eyeballs demanded, holding the gun upward again, readying for another blow.

Vanessa desperately tried to think of a way to intercede, but No-Neck pushed her forward.

"Let's get them both in the room before you kill him and Boss kills *us*."

Eyeballs grunted, then muttered something as he yanked Dylan to his feet. "When it's time to kill you—and, oh, there will be a time—it'll be my pleasure."

"Nice fantasy life you've got there."

No-Neck cut the ties on Dylan's feet but left the hand ones on. Then Eyeballs practically lifted Dylan off his feet. Dylan was launched forward, falling into the room they'd been in, and with his hands tied he had no way to stop the forward momentum. He crashed into the wall, falling to the ground with a loud thud.

Vanessa struggled against No-Neck's grasp, and when he let her go she rushed to Dylan's side.

"God. *God.* Are you okay? Are you…?" She struggled to move him onto his back so she could see how hurt he was. She didn't even notice the door close or the loud thud of the lock, so intent she was on helping Dylan.

He didn't groan as she rolled him over, and she might have thought he'd passed out, but his eyes were open and on her. His mouth was quirked as if this were a joke. Gingerly, she touched all the bruises and scratches on his stubbled face.

She shouldn't have done it—somewhere in the back of her mind the real Vanessa was losing it over the fact she was gently caressing Dylan Delaney's face.

But her fingers brushed through his hair of their own accord. Gently, she cupped his wounded jaw. "Are you okay?"

His gaze, so direct and serious, did some strange things to the spaces inside her heart. She wanted to look away, but her pride was at stake. That's what kept her gaze locked to his. Pride. Nothing else.

"If I say no, are you going to kiss it and make it better?"

She knew she should jerk away or cuss him out, but she couldn't bring her fingers away from the silky texture of his hair. "You've got to stop pissing them off. You won't survive."

He leaned into her touch, and something flopped in her chest. "I'll survive. And keep you safe while I do it."

"I can handle myself, Dylan."

He made a noncommittal noise, then pulled his hands out from behind his back.

"Hey, how'd you get out of that?" she demanded, staring openmouthed at the plastic bindings that had fallen to the floor.

He grinned at her, and she saw the red marks around his mouth where the tape had been did nothing to dim the potency of that grin. "Magic."

HE WANTED TO touch her. Hell, he wanted to kiss her. The pain in his stomach was nothing compared to the gentle comfort of her hands on him. On his face and in his hair. Her hair fell over him, a tangled dark mess, and nothing about her was different from how it had ever been—tattoos, wary eyes, hard mouth.

Except her touch was light, and in this strange kidnapped world, he didn't feel like Dylan Delaney, where the eyes of Bent and his father fit like a suit two sizes too small.

She, and he, felt right. Together they had the power to weather this odd storm. For a moment, brief and changing, he *knew* she felt that too.

And then she pulled away.

Which was fine. What could be done during a kidnapping? Not much. He was grateful she seemed more like herself. Sturdier and sharper, instead of lost and hazy. Maybe her memory was still fuzzy, but the blow to the head hopefully hadn't caused any problems with the pregnancy.

He sat up, not at all perturbed by the fact that she watched him with frustration simmering in her gaze.

"You have to tell me. The fighting. The getting out of duct tape and ties and…you have to tell me how *you* of all people know how to be—be—"

"Fiercely lethal?"

She rolled her eyes, but she didn't offer another term.

He sighed. Not more than forty-eight hours ago, revealing his secrets to anyone—let alone a Carson—would have felt like life and death. But now he understood life and death in a way he hadn't even as a sniper.

Because it wasn't facing death that had changed him, it was facing *life*. The moment she'd told him she was pregnant, he'd been handed new life and everything he thought he'd known had flipped. All the things he'd thought mattered dissolved. He didn't care what anyone thought of him. Not even his father. Because he'd created a life…and whether he fully grasped that yet, he knew this child would be the center of his life. Part of him. Always.

So it didn't matter if Vanessa knew. It didn't matter if she told everyone when they got back home—and it was *when* not *if* they got back home, in his mind.

"Well, all that college bragging my father did to you in that last memory of yours…"

She pushed a finger to her head, near the bump where she'd fallen. Her eyebrows drew together and he got to his feet.

"You remember?"

"No. Not exactly. But it doesn't feel like… Even though I can't put it all on a clear timeline, that doesn't feel as close to now as it did. I still can't believe Laurel and Grady are *married*, but it doesn't seem… I feel like I remember them together. Being irritated at them together. She's a cop. I remember the uniform. I remember her holding a gun, I think. Maybe."

"There's been some trouble the past year or so. You'd likely have seen her draw her weapon a few times."

"Trouble? What kind of trouble? Is everyone…?"

He could see the fear and horror chase over her features as she realized she might not remember losing someone she loved.

"As far as I know, every Carson you care about is present and accounted for."

She swallowed. "Right." Then her eyes narrowed. "You're trying to distract me."

"You're distracting yourself. I don't even have

to try." He folded his arms behind his head and smiled at her.

She growled. "*How* do you know how to fight and escape bonds? Jump out of vans and incapacitate dudes with guns?"

He figured he needed to be straight and simple, so they could move on to far more important matters. Like Adele's possible role and the small plan he had for escaping tonight once he got some more info.

"I didn't go to college. I made everyone think I did. Took the money for tuition, told Dad I wanted to handle all my bills to learn how to be responsible. I forged transcripts and report cards and enlisted in the army and became a sniper instead."

"You…" She gaped at him like a landed fish. "You… That's a lie. That… You couldn't have. Why? Why go through all the trouble?"

"I knew I had seven years. Graduate high school early, take five years for undergrad, claim the need for a masters for another two, maybe three if I could stretch it. So, that's what I made them think. I knew if I did what I wanted in that short period of time, I could come back and be everything he wanted me to be. I just had to go be *me* first."

"Dylan. That's crazy."

"No. It felt like that's what I had to do. Cam

refused the bank, Laurel was always meant to be a cop, and Jen didn't have the patience for finance. She just wanted to run the store. I was the only one left."

"Considering your father's going to live to be three million since he's evil incarnate, I'd say he was enough left."

Dylan shook his head. "No. I was the only true Bent Delaney left to take the mantle. The bank has been in our family since it began. Direct eldest son to eldest son. I'm not the eldest, but Cam wouldn't take it. You have to understand family pressure, Vanessa. Carson and Delaney pressure. We are what our names are." And yet, wasn't he sitting here thinking none of it mattered anymore?

Maybe it didn't. Maybe it did. The *now* didn't matter in the story, because it was the choice he'd made. It was what he'd felt then.

"You went into the army, became a sniper, falsified your *life* for seven years. That's *insane*. You're talking like it was the only choice."

"For me, it was."

"You could have told your father what you wanted to do."

"No. It wasn't an option. I was coming back. I was going to take on my responsibility. But I needed a few years to…" It sounded stupid to say *find myself*. But that's what he'd needed. He'd needed to know who he was outside of Bent. Outside of numbers and appearances.

Cam had gone to the marines, and Dylan hadn't been allowed to follow. So he'd found a different way. Maybe he should have stood up to his father, but he'd been seventeen.

The bottom line was, he hadn't. "I needed it to be secret. I needed to be someone not connected to this place. I can't explain why I needed it, only that I did. And it shaped me, made me, gave me the time I needed to be able to come home and take that…" *Noose.* Following his father's footsteps felt like a noose he couldn't escape.

"I had my me time, then I came home to fulfill my role as a Delaney. It was a little out of the box, but it wasn't insane."

"Army. A *sniper.* I…" She shook her head and paced around the room. "That's a lot of work for risking your life for your country. You faked your life to sacrifice yourself, to protect. I don't understand that."

He cocked his head and studied her. She didn't realize it, but she'd put her hand over her stomach. He thought she was finally beginning to believe the pregnancy was real. That he was the father.

"I think you're starting to," he said gently.

She looked down at her hand, then dropped it. She kept her back to him, and he couldn't read her posture so he crossed to her. Gently, knowing she'd probably fight him off, he put his hands on her shoulders.

When she didn't move away and didn't even tense under his fingers, he turned her to face him.

Her eyes were direct, though there was something in them he couldn't read. Suspicion maybe. Or possibly just confusion. She didn't understand him.

That didn't hurt his feelings though. She was a Carson. He was a Delaney. They'd never understand each other.

But, God, he wanted to. Understand her. Have her understand him. He wanted to chase this *power* that arced between them. But it wasn't the time or place. Maybe it'd never be, but definitely not now. "Right now, we'll focus on getting out of here."

When the tension crept into her shoulders, he squeezed. "Don't worry. I'll protect you. I'm an expert."

She didn't laugh or even crack a smile, but the moment held. And in that moment he needed her to believe that he'd protect her with everything he was.

He placed his own hand over her stomach, nerves and fear of the future jumping through every part of him. He didn't let it show in his expression though. "I'll protect you both."

She took a sharp breath in, then slowly let it

out. Then her hand reached out and cupped his jaw, just as she had when he'd been sprawled on the floor after crashing into the wall. His chest clutched, a metal fist squeezing against his heart and then his lungs.

Her dark eyes were rich and deep and fathomless. He saw something he'd never seen in her before. Warmth. Care.

You're losing it, Delaney.

"Protect all three of us," she whispered and then pressed her mouth to his.

Chapter Twelve

The kiss was a mistake. Out of place in every possible way.

But Vanessa wrapped her arms around Dylan's neck and took it deeper anyway. Her whole life had been built on out-of-place mistakes. She *was* an out-of-place mistake. Her philosophy had always been, why not embrace it?

So she lost herself in a kiss she shouldn't have allowed herself, and figured that was vintage Vanessa.

Until Dylan took control, his hands sliding over her cheeks and into her hair, fingers tangling there, changing the angle of the kiss as his tongue swept across her lips, then invaded her mouth.

Now she understood why his hands were big and rough and capable. Maybe it still didn't make sense to her, a secret life, a secret self, but she understood all the incongruous things about him now.

She knew something about him no one else

did. In this moment, they were experiencing something together that no one would be able to share with them. They were linked. Connected.

And she wanted him. So why not take?

Slowly, oh so slowly, he ended the kiss. Pulled away just enough to keep their mouths apart, but her body was still pressed to his. Their heartbeats thudded against each other as their gazes met.

She'd expected to see...*horror* wasn't the right word, but something close to it. Regret. Disgust. She was a Carson and he was a Delaney. He'd only ever see her as a mistake. Even without all her memory, she knew that.

She had the flash of him walking out of her apartment above her shop, looking rumpled and angry. Disgusted. At the time she'd thought it was with her, but somehow in this moment, she realized it was with himself. With his loss of control.

Because his image was the gift he'd given his family, even when it wasn't him at all.

"Dylan." She wanted to kiss him again. Comfort him for...something. Offer understanding, maybe, even though her understanding was limited.

But then she realized she could picture her apartment. She knew what color her sheets were and that she lived there.

"Wait. Wait." She could't analyze why he didn't look horrified now, only the fact that she knew...

"I—I run the mechanic shop, not just help out. I run it. I live above it." She struggled to keep that thread of memory, holding tight to him as if he was her anchor, even as she looked blindly at his chest. "It's mine now, because—because Grady helped me buy it after Jim croaked." She swallowed. She could picture some of the cars she'd worked on. Could feel herself walking down the boardwalk from her shop to Rightful Claim.

Where Grady didn't live anymore. Because he'd married Laurel. They'd gotten together when their stepbrother had been accused of murder and Grady and Laurel had worked together to clear Clint's name. They'd fallen in love and pissed off a lot of people.

She looked up at Dylan's dark gaze, amazed parts of her memory had returned.

"You should probably kiss me again," Dylan suggested, pulling her closer.

At her sharp look, he shrugged, a grin flirting at the corner of his mouth. "What? It made you remember. Might jog some more pieces."

Her mouth curved, suggestive words about to tumble out of her mouth, no matter where they were or what they were facing.

But the door flung open, and afterward, Vanessa realized there was something telling about the fact she and Dylan didn't jump apart. She didn't know what, but it meant, well, something that they held on to each other instead.

But it was something they'd have to figure out later because Adele was pushed into the room. Her hair was disheveled, and there was a trickle of blood coming out of her nose.

Dylan immediately rushed to her side. Vanessa stayed put.

Blood or not, she didn't trust the woman with the icy eyes. Because though she made odd, almost crying noises, Vanessa didn't see any tears.

"Got a call with the boss," No-Neck growled. "You three stay in here. Plot your escape because I'd love to break your kneecaps in the process."

Dylan ignored No-Neck and Eyeballs as they cackled and shut the door.

"Are you all right?" he asked Adele, gentleness in his tone, in his touch.

Vanessa scowled.

"I just..." Adele swallowed, her hand shaking as she brought it up to her nose. "I did everything they said, but they're so rough." She made another little crying sound. Still no tears.

Vanessa went over to the box of tissues on the desk and handed it to Adele. Adele blinked at the proffered box and then daintily took one.

"Oh, I..." She dabbed it at her nose and squeezed her eyes shut. "I get a little faint when I see blood."

"It's all right," Dylan assured her.

Vanessa barely resisted the urge to roll her eyes. She wouldn't have cared for the fainting-damsel act in the best of circumstances, but considering Adele'd watched Dylan get slammed by the butt of a gun repeatedly with little reaction, Vanessa was having a hard time working up sympathy.

Of course, Dylan was trained to get beat up and keep fighting. A secret soldier. Dylan Delaney.

And she was the only one who knew. Something about that felt important, and it softened her enough to crouch down and clean up Adele's nose for her.

"There. Good as new. Just tilt your head forward and pinch it right at the bridge. Should be right as rain in a few."

Adele winced and did as Vanessa instructed.

Dylan raised an eyebrow at her. "Bloody-nose expert?"

"I'm a Carson. Of *course* I'm a bloody-nose expert. My own. My brother's. My cousins'. It's like a virtual parade of bloody noses from getting punched in the face." Vanessa turned her attention back to Adele. "You weren't punched in the face though, were you?"

"Oh, I…" Her hand fluttered restlessly in the air. "No. They pushed me around a bit and I…"

"Looks more like an elevation nosebleed to

me," Vanessa observed, ignoring Dylan's censuring look.

"Oh, but I fell. They pushed me and I fell."

Vanessa got to her feet and shrugged. "If you say so."

"They said they have some meeting with their boss," Adele said, clearly trying to change the subject. "And they needed that room. Do you think whoever is behind this is coming here?" Her voice vibrated with concern.

Vanessa managed to swallow what she wanted to say: *I think their boss is already here, liar.*

She didn't want to believe Dylan was falling for Adele's flittering fragile-female crap, but he was so gentle when he helped Adele to her feet and then led her to the chair he'd put Vanessa in not that long ago. He picked up the suit jacket he'd placed over her lap earlier, and put it on Adele's.

"Just take it easy. Whoever their boss is can't be that dangerous, or he wouldn't have hired two muscle-bound goons to do his dirty work for him."

"Do you really think?" Adele replied, eyes big and something like adoring on Dylan.

He patted her shoulder. "Yes, I do. Trust me. The only thing we need to worry about is the fact those two have guns."

Vanessa didn't care for the oily black slick of jealousy running through her. She was starting to think Dylan's gentle caretaking wasn't because he cared about her or even their baby. No, this was just who he was. Vanessa wasn't special at all.

Well, except for that kiss.

"You also need to worry about the fact Eyeballs has a penchant for kicking your butt," Vanessa said to Dylan. Because it was its own kind of pain to see all the physical evidence of their brutal way with Dylan, even if he acted as though it was nothing.

Dylan sent Vanessa a sharp look. "I'm fine. We'll all be fine." He turned his attention back to Adele. "I promise you that."

Vanessa was not a jealous woman, or at least she hadn't been. But it burned in her now. Which pissed her off. At Dylan. At Adele. At No-Neck and Eyeballs out there. But mostly at herself.

Adele grasped for Dylan's hand, squeezing when she found it. "I feel so much better being in here with you two. It's awful being alone, not knowing what's going to happen."

"You don't have an idea or two of what they might be after?" Vanessa asked, hoping to sound innocent rather than sarcastic. "I mean, you've had more time with them. We escaped. Of course, you weren't in the back of the van with us." She smiled blandly.

"I was in the front," Adele said, letting Dylan's hand go and dabbing at her nose with the tissue again. "Tied up in the front seat. Only one person could fit, and they needed me to navigate. You were knocked out and Dylan was...uncooperative." She stumbled a bit over the words, and Vanessa thought it sounded rehearsed, but she had a practiced, simple excuse. Vanessa had to give Adele that.

"How'd you get in the van without us seeing you?" Dylan asked. There was speculation in his tone, but his voice was gentle.

"They took me out the front before they ever came into the back, at least that I can figure. I sat tied up in that van for I don't know how long before they returned and drove off."

It was a quick and plausible explanation. Vanessa scowled. This woman was a pro liar, that was for sure. Vanessa could tell Dylan was doubting her involvement, but Vanessa refused to entertain doubts. Sometimes you had to be hard and unyielding to get what you wanted.

She wanted her freedom and Dylan's safety.

Maybe you just want Dylan.

Well, maybe she did. But she couldn't get anything she wanted until they were home, safe in Bent, with only family curses to threaten them.

DYLAN WASN'T IMMUNE to Vanessa's speculative gaze. He understood it, even. The evidence pointed to Adele.

But was it too easy to put the blame on Adele? Dylan had the feeling something else had to be behind this. Maybe Adele really was being forced to cooperate, and since she was willing and not fighting, she was given certain things like a change of clothes.

Dylan knew Adele. He'd trusted her with the bank. He couldn't quite accept she was wholly behind this. Vanessa didn't know Adele personally, even if she was starting to remember more.

Something warm and very dangerous filled him at the thought of that kiss, of those memories. He wasn't foolish or romantic enough to think his kiss had unlocked her memories in a scientific sense, but it was nice to pretend.

Not the time or place though. Adele was shaking.

Well, if he sat back on his haunches and analyzed it the way Vanessa was, with some cynicism and suspicion, it was more that same vibration as when she'd sat next to him on the couch during the phone call. It reminded him more of excitement than nerves.

But people expressed nerves differently. He still had enough soldier in him to know he couldn't judge people's reactions by his own. Before he'd made sniper, there'd been a fellow soldier who'd giggled whenever they got into trouble in basic. Not because he was happy, but because nerves made him laugh.

That kid hadn't made it through, but remembering it reminded Dylan that not everyone could control and hone their reactions to danger. More so, not everyone reacted in a way that made any sense.

Still, Adele's actions struck him as off, and he was still enough of a soldier to be wary of behavior that didn't make sense or follow a pattern.

Fear didn't always, of course. People didn't always. But he'd be wary until he found something concrete to believe in. Wary didn't mean cruel. It meant careful.

It wasn't like he could go by Vanessa's clear Adele-is-evil judgment. Vanessa had made a life out of distrusting people from the outset.

It irritated him that his own radar was compromised by knowing Adele for so long and not really ever *getting* to know her. She was Adele Oscar. Bank employee. He knew her attitudes about customers and the cleanliness of the teller station or her shared office, but nothing about how she'd act in crisis or what her background was that would inform her reactions.

Dylan couldn't let frustration lead him though. He had to focus on the task at hand, even if Adele was a wild card he couldn't pin down.

They needed an escape plan. And three against

two was better than two against two. Especially when two on one side were armed, and one on the other side was pregnant.

"If they needed her to navigate, she knows where we are," Vanessa pointed out, not kindly. "We only need to find a way to have her make a phone call to get help up here." She sent Adele a challenging smirk.

Adele's eyes went wide. "I don't know where we are. Not really. Not enough to lead someone here." She grasped for Dylan's hand again, and he let her find it and squeeze.

"You could give them everything you know," Dylan said gently. "If we could get access to a phone, we can call my sister. Even with just some clues, the police would be able to track us down, if they haven't already pinged your phone."

"Pinged my…? Oh, maybe, but they made me turn it off. It's only been on when we made our phone call."

"Well, that doesn't mean we can't get a phone call in, and you can tell the police everything you remember seeing on the drive up here."

"It was dark," Adele said weakly.

"No. Not that dark," Dylan countered, extracting his hand from hers. She should be excited about the possibility of getting them out of here. Not shrinking away from it. No reaction to fear would make a person refuse to help them escape.

He stood and moved next to Vanessa.

"I don't know… I can't remember." She looked up at him pleadingly.

Dylan couldn't find compassion for her when she wouldn't even try to help. He narrowed his eyes at her. She swallowed audibly and even scooted back in the chair.

"Think," he ordered sharply. "Tell me everything you remember, no matter how insignificant it seems. But we'll start at the beginning. After they left the bank, which way out of Bent did they go?"

Adele blinked, her eyes darting everywhere. Her hands fluttered until she linked them over her lap. She took a deep breath. "I'm really not good under pressure," she whispered.

He'd seen her deal with difficult customers. Large, angry men who thought they deserved a loan, or a customer wanting a check to be cashed even if they didn't have the proper identification.

She'd never crumbled under pressure then. Either there was more to the story than she was telling them, or she was behind this. Either way, he'd be calm but firm. Until he knew for sure.

"All I'm asking you to do is describe what you saw, where you went. No one's going to blame you if you don't remember everything perfectly."

Adele nodded vigorously, twisting her fingers

together. "Okay. Okay. I was afraid, Dylan. So afraid." She looked up at him, tears in her blue eyes.

They were meant to stir up sympathy, and it worked. He softened, even as he could all but feel Vanessa hardening next to him. Adele shrunk back in her seat, clearly intimidated by Vanessa's cold glare.

So Dylan stepped in front of Vanessa, a kind of shield. For both of them really. Vanessa could bore holes into his back, and he could hopefully find a way to get through to Adele. "You just take it easy and tell me what you remember."

Adele sniffled and nodded. "Okay. Okay. So. They started driving. Out of the front parking lot, but instead of getting on the highway, they drove down Ellington toward the back of town."

Dylan nodded. He'd figured that part out himself. He'd managed to pay attention to the turns in the back of the van, but measuring distance was harder since he hadn't been able to determine how fast they were going. He had a feeling he'd been lost the minute they'd gotten out of town.

"Then they went north, I think. I'm not good with direction."

"What road after Ellington?"

She pushed her fingers to her temples. "I-I'm not sure. I was just terrified. I wasn't paying attention. Those guns." She shuddered. "I never thought I was squeamish about guns, but they're so—so—"

"The roads, Adele. Let's focus on the roads. Ellington to the back of town then north?" He didn't think they'd gone north based on the sun's positioning when they'd escaped, but he'd draw out what she claimed to remember anyway.

"Country Road B maybe? Yes, I think that might be it. North toward the Tetons, maybe? It'd be isolated." She pressed her fist to her mouth. "We're *so* isolated," she whispered, a tear falling over and onto her cheek.

This time it didn't soften him. Everything she told him was the exact opposite of his own theories, his own gut reactions. He'd been paying attention. They'd gone to the back of town, then south. Not toward the national park.

Maybe he should trust the woman who'd seen it all, but Dylan couldn't bring himself to compromise what he *knew* in his gut to what someone he didn't trust claimed.

They *were* in the mountains though, and this nice cabin was more suited for Jackson Hole than anything south of Bent.

Maybe his instincts had been off. He had been beaten pretty badly. It could have messed up his sense of direction.

Hell. This was a mess. He didn't like second-guessing himself. Second-guessing got you killed in war, and this wasn't all that different from war.

"She's so full of it," Vanessa whispered into his ear.

Dylan gave Vanessa a sharp look. She returned it with a baleful one of her own. Because she'd been out of sorts—physically and in the memory department—and they were kidnapped and all, he'd somewhat forgotten her normal personality of doing the exact opposite of what anyone asked of her.

"Excuse us a second." He took Vanessa's arm and moved her to the far corner. They were all still in the same room, but if he kept his voice low, surely they could have a conversation Adele wouldn't overhear.

He huddled with Vanessa, lowering his mouth to her ear so he could whisper. "It isn't fair to hold her to our standards."

"What does *that* mean?" Vanessa retorted, crossing her arms over her chest. She kept her voice low, but she didn't whisper.

He kept whispering. "It means you grew up a Carson, and I was in the army. We're not exactly *normal*."

He could tell she took some offense to that, and probably wanted to argue with him that they weren't at all similar, but she didn't. She sucked in a breath and let it out, then glared over his shoulder at Adele. "She's fishy, one way or another." That one she definitely whispered.

He glanced over his shoulder at Adele. She was looking at them intently, but based on the confused line between her eyebrows, he didn't think she was getting most of the conversation.

"I agree with you on that, but that doesn't mean we can just leave her here. Any escape plan has to involve her, even if we don't trust her."

"There's too much goody-goody Delaney in you."

He managed a smile. "Some things you can't shake."

Her brown eyes met his, and he saw something venturing on soft there in the edges if he looked closely. Very, very closely. "Like feuds and curses?" she asked carefully.

He couldn't resist dropping his forehead to hers. "Like who we are, underneath all that." And underneath all that, he thought they could maybe be something.

But first, they had to escape.

Chapter Thirteen

Back in Bent, Adele Oscar's house

"Nothing." Laurel couldn't keep the disgust out of her voice. They'd gotten the search warrant to go through Adele Oscar's residence and so far had come up with nothing. Meanwhile, the seconds ticked down and Dylan, Vanessa and Adele were still missing.

She hadn't slept last night. She'd convinced herself it was because she was anxiously awaiting the search warrant to come through or something from the phone company about a location hit on Adele's cell. She was worried about her brother and sister-in-law, so tension and sleeplessness could only be wrapped up in work and fear.

Surely it wasn't over the silent, stilted dinner she'd shared with her husband last night. That was just anxiety. They were both worried about their siblings. It was natural there'd be this wall between them. Grady and his cousins were probably breaking laws trying to find Vanessa, while she was toeing the law's line trying to find them.

But they'd gone to bed and turned away from each other, and it had eaten at her all night.

She closed her eyes and rubbed her hands over her face. On the job wasn't the time to think about her emotions or her marriage.

"You okay?" Hart asked, a note of gentleness in his voice. "You're looking a little, as my mother would say, peaked."

She opened her eyes to give Hart a sharp, fierce look. "I'm fine."

He shrugged. "If you say so, boss."

"I'm not your boss," she grumbled, closing Adele's hall-closet door, which contained nothing but meticulously organized coats and shoes.

"No, but you're grooming me," Hart said conversationally, taking off the latex gloves he'd used to poke through the trash.

"I'm not," she protested, probably stupidly. She was irritated he'd figured her out but also impressed. She'd been trying to be subtle, though that had never been her strong point.

"You've let me take the lead on almost everything. Laurel, I've worked with you enough years. You never let anyone take the lead without a very specific reason, and this is your *brother*. There's no way you'd let me take the lead without a reason. You're grooming me."

She let out a sigh. It would have been nice for him to keep thinking he was just her help, but he'd figured it out. That was good, all in all. "Okay, I'm grooming you."

"Leaving us?" he asked, his voice devoid of any tell. Also impressive. He'd grown a lot in the past few years. She felt a kind of older-sister pride in that.

"Temporarily."

Hart raised his eyebrows. "Never thought I'd see the day you'd…" He'd need to work on his poker face, because when he finally figured things out, his eyes got a little wide as it all clicked.

"Oh. *Oh.* Well, I guess congratulations are in order."

"We've got a ways to go till congratulations are in order. It's still early and no one at the department knows yet."

He frowned. "They should know, Laurel."

"You sound like my husband."

"And you're irritated I do because you know we're both right. They should know, and you shouldn't be running yourself so hard. Pretty sure you should be on desk duty."

She might have gotten bent out of shape about Hart of all people scolding her, but there was one simple truth to this case. "My brother and sister-in-law are missing and in danger. I can't step back. I'm taking care of myself. You're here, aren't you?"

"I'm here. It's wild though. You and a Carson. Your brother and another Carson." He shook his head.

"What? You think the whole town is going to fall down around our ears?" She asked it too sharply and with too much of her own baggage weighing the words down. *Idiot.* She needed to get ahold of her personal ties to this case. Pregnant or not, family or not, she had to be the detective this case needed.

But Hart didn't flinch or evade. He smiled kindly. "Nah. Just crumble at the edges a little bit. Maybe a few more kidnappings and fires. Mob might come through and get me shot again. But eventually Satan and hellfire will get bored. Bent doesn't die."

She laughed a little at the Satan-and-hellfire bit, but it hardly felt far off. They'd had a lot of trouble over the last year. It had started before her and Grady but not by much. Most of the trouble happened after.

She did *not* believe in curses. Or feuds. At all.

On a deep breath, she repeated Hart's words to herself. Bent didn't die. Through all the trouble, even the trouble they were knee-deep in, Bent kept living, and so did its people. Even if there were curses, Bent would weather them all.

And so will we, she thought to herself, twisting her wedding ring on her finger.

"Let's get ready to go." But first she'd send a text to Grady. She pulled out her phone, surprised to find one from him already there.

Taking care of yourself & co, princess?

She smiled at the & co, and what she knew was a tentative peace offering. She decided to offer one of her own.

Doing my best. I'm going to knock off early. Take a nap.

Real nap or metaphorical nap?

Depends. What time can you be home?

I'll beat you there.

Simple as that, she was settled again, centered. She'd married a good man. He'd married a good woman. And whoever was crazy enough to kidnap a Carson and Delaney together was definitely going to come out with the raw end of this deal.

"Ready?" Hart asked.

Laurel looked around the living room. "Yes. We've been through everything, and I think I'm going to take the afternoon off. You can handle things for a while—call the phone company again and again if you have to. We've got to get something on that ping, but my brain's mush. I need a few hours." She started for the door, but then she stopped at a little desk in the corner. They'd gone through it looking for clues and hadn't found any. But she realized, now that they'd been through the whole house, the little stack of paint samples and fabric swatches on top of the desk didn't actually match anything done inside the house.

"Hart. Look at this."

"Yeah." He picked them up. "Paint samples and fabric swatches. You think she's planning on coming into some ransom money to redecorate?"

"Could be, but things have been marked off. Chosen." She didn't say anything else and instead waited, wondering if he'd come to the same conclusion she was coming to.

"But…" He looked around the living room they stood in. He took the time to walk around the entire house again, studying fabrics and paints in contrast to the samples he held in his hand.

"This isn't for here," he finally said, certain.

"No. She has another residence. Or had one built. Recently."

"A new cabin, perhaps? Like the one your father described Dylan sitting in the middle of, with Adele Oscar silent and scared next to him?"

Laurel kept pulling the thread. "Surely she wouldn't be so stupid as to kidnap someone to a cabin in her own name. And we checked all the new constructs in the area. We didn't see her name."

"But she put herself on camera. Made herself look like a victim. We'll expand our search now that we've got a name and a reason to," Hart said, sounding suitably in charge. "But there are other options here."

"Like what? If she's redecorating, it's *her* place." Laurel began to think of all the ways that could be untrue, but she waited for Hart to explain his own theories.

"Two possibilities. First, it's her place but it's not under her name—at least the name we have. What if she bought it under another name? A name attached to a bank account where ransom money couldn't be detected."

"God, that's far-fetched." And possible. So completely possible.

"It could also be under a boyfriend's name. Or a family member's. She could have a stake in it without her name being on the papers."

A boyfriend. There was definitely no evidence of one, and the people at the bank they'd talked to couldn't list any friends she might have spent time with outside of banker hours.

But the bank.

"There's a third option."

Hart snapped his fingers. "She works at a bank and handles home loans."

Laurel nodded. "Let's see if we can subpoena some bank records."

Chapter Fourteen

Vanessa wanted to escape this cabin because of the men with guns and whatnot, but at this point she also wanted to escape because she was going absolutely stir-crazy.

"Can't you just take them out?" she demanded irritably of Dylan as he went over the layout of the cabin with Adele again, trying to understand the full scale and find weak points for escape, or so he said.

Adele gave Vanessa a speculative look and Dylan gave her a censuring one. He still didn't want anyone to know about his secret. It made her want to scream. Partly because it was a stupid secret, and partly because they were kidnapped and who *cared*? Let everyone know that with a gun in his hand, Dylan Delaney could pick off anyone standing in their way.

"They have guns. We don't," Dylan said simply.

"We only need one," Vanessa returned.

"They'd still have one. We can't risk it."

Dylan's patient, indulgent tone pissed her off, even if he was right.

Right and protective and sweet somehow. It made no earthly sense that a part of her wanted him to bust into army-sniper mode, and another ached for the man who thought he had to hide himself because of his name and Bent. She felt the second on a much deeper level than she wanted to.

She didn't have secrets. Bent and her family knew who she was…sort of. Maybe she'd cultivated a big-mouth, rough and dangerous, say-anything personality because she felt like she had to in order to survive being a Carson—especially a female Carson. You had to be hard and you had to be rough, or you had to leave. Hadn't her aunt disappeared and not talked to the family for years? She hadn't fit the mold—so instead of trying to fight that, she'd escaped.

Vanessa had done everything she could to fit the mold, even when she hadn't particularly felt as rough-and-tumble as she was supposed to be. She'd probably cut off some fingers before she'd willingly show any soft side to her family or to Bent in general.

"Maybe we should ask for food," Adele suggested brightly. "It might help everyone's mood."

Vanessa sent her the dirtiest look she had in

her arsenal. Maybe she *was* hungry and irritable, but that didn't mean she appreciated Adele pointing it out.

"Good idea," Dylan said, striding over to the door. He began pounding on it until No-Neck appeared, growling and vicious.

"You need to feed us," Dylan demanded. "It'd be easier if you gave us some snacks and water to keep in here."

"Yeah, I'm real worried about your easy, pal," No-Neck returned with a snort, but he eyed Adele and then Vanessa. "Only because Boss's orders are to keep you alive and well. You'll come with me. I ain't your chef." He gripped Dylan's arm and yanked him out of the room.

Well, Dylan allowed himself to be yanked, Vanessa thought. He'd had that furious, violent look on his face, but then he'd tightened his jaw and banked it. She noted he couldn't seem to sweet-talk the guards, but he'd feign weakness for them.

She realized it was because he was used to one and not the other. He was always feigning weakness and never trying to sweet-talk anyone.

That flutter was back around her heart. Like she was impressed with him or something. Like he kind of amazed her and she wanted...

Well, it didn't matter what else she wanted

right now. Just freedom. That was all that mattered at the moment.

Adele began to wander around the room in Dylan's absence. She touched a chair, poked at the wall. Her gaze went to the ceiling, the high, narrow windows.

It was dark, Vanessa noted. They'd been here two days now, with almost no sleep, and that was after their uncomfortable night in the woods.

She had to believe people were working to find them, but this was an awful long time not to be found.

"I didn't realize you and Dylan were so… chummy," Adele offered. A casual observation, or so Adele wanted Vanessa to believe.

Vanessa snorted from her seat in the desk chair. She was feeling a little queasy again, though not as weak. Adele walking in relative circles had her closing her eyes against the round of dizziness she could now remember was just one of her lucky pregnancy symptoms. "Chummy?"

"Is that not the word for it?" Adele chuckled. "There's certainly a connection between you two. An energy."

"Energy," Vanessa muttered with some disgust, opening one eye hesitantly.

Adele had stopped her prowling so she was standing in front of Vanessa. She leaned close, as if they were two girlfriends conspiring with each other. "It just crackles in the air."

"It's called hate," Vanessa returned flatly. Adele was fishing, and Vanessa wasn't about to be the trout she landed.

"You're pregnant," Adele said gently.

Vanessa gave Adele a steely look while she fought the urge to touch her stomach. "Not by a damn Delaney."

Adele rolled her eyes. "I never understood this town's obsession with Carsons and Delaneys. You're just people, like the rest of us."

Vanessa noticed she said *this town*. Maybe it was just the way she spoke, but it gave Vanessa a tingling jolt of excitement. Maybe they weren't that far outside of Bent if Adele was referring to *this town*.

"Besides, you two were wound around each other like vines when I was thrown in here. You can't tell me something isn't going on. Or maybe you just don't remember."

Still fishing for information. Assessing Vanessa's memory and relationship with Dylan with every question, every glance. Why would she need to know the nature of her relationship with Dylan or the state of her memory if she wasn't gathering information for something?

"It's an awful bump. Not recognizing people. Pregnancy. Quite a trauma."

"I'll live," Vanessa replied.

"Of course." Adele sighed gustily. "As soon as we get out of here."

"A shame you can't help that along."

"We can't all be like you, Vanessa. So strong and sure of ourselves. We can't all be Carsons and Delaneys in Bent. That would get a bit incestuous, wouldn't it?"

There was an edge to her voice and Vanessa wanted to smirk. She thought with the right attitude, the right throwaway comments, she might actually be able to break Adele into showing her true colors.

"And yet Carsons and Delaneys are all Bent seems to care about," Vanessa said with a sweet smile. "The world spins on and on, and all the citizens can seem to care about is Grady and Laurel getting married. Old man Delaney having an affair with a *married* Carson all those years ago."

Inspired, Vanessa blinked her wide eyes at Adele. "Oh, Mr. Delaney. I'd guess you worked more closely with him than Dylan, before Dylan came home."

Adele's face was perfectly blank, but everything about her was tense. Vanessa let her smile go sly and wide.

"I work with everyone at the bank," Adele said, in something like a robot voice. No inflection, no emotion.

"Sure, but Mr. Delaney is the boss. The head honcho. Surely there's some need to please the guy in charge?"

Adele's jaw twitched and her hand curled into a fist before she quickly released it. "I do my job. I've always done my job."

It was there, somewhere under the control—a breaking point. And it centered on that job. Vanessa only had to find it.

But Dylan returned just then with some food—more horrendous pizza pockets—and a few bottles of water.

Vanessa kept her attention on Adele. All that speculation, that intent staring and incessant questioning? Gone. The anger and tension melted away.

She was playing some kind of role, and Dylan was falling for it hook, line and sinker.

Men.

Vanessa couldn't even hate him for it because she knew it stemmed from that innate Delaney goodness. He wanted there to be good in the world, and he wanted to believe the people in his life were that.

Vanessa wanted to blame it on arrogance and the fact he just couldn't believe someone who'd worked for his family for a decade was bad, because that would make his initial estimation about

Adele wrong. A few days ago she *would* have blamed it on that.

But it wasn't that. He wanted her to be good because thinking people were bad was always his last resort. *Unless it has to do with Carsons.*

True enough, and yet he'd jumped to help Vanessa herself, taken care of her, protected her this whole time. Maybe at some point she'd convince herself it was just because of the accidental pregnancy.

But the kiss from earlier was too fresh in her mind. Dylan Delaney had fallen for *her* and was going to believe she was good regardless of all evidence to the contrary.

She swallowed, looking away from Adele to the man in question. He handed her a pizza pocket, wrapped up in a paper towel. This one was cooked through. He placed the bottle of water, already opened, on the desk next to her.

It was a gesture that, anywhere else, would have pissed her off. Why didn't it here?

"I think I have a plan," Dylan stated.

With that, Vanessa didn't have time to figure it out.

"DON'T YOU THINK—"

Dylan already knew what Vanessa was going to say. Now, while he explained the plan, after the fact. She'd hate the plan simply by merit of her safety being paramount—and added to the fact he was going to tell Adele?

Yeah, he expected fireworks.

Hopefully, he'd learned how to deal with Vanessa's fireworks, because he was pretty sure he could pull this off.

"Those two idiots out there?" Dylan said, nodding his head toward the door and ignoring Vanessa's protests. "They *love* to talk to each other. They practically wrote down their evening routine for me."

"Just because we know their routine doesn't mean we could escape and then know where to go." Adele flicked a look at Vanessa. "I doubt a pregnant woman should be running around in the dark woods."

"You'd be surprised what a pregnant woman is capable of," Vanessa returned, her voice a low growl.

Dylan grinned at her. "*Very* surprised," Dylan agreed. "Plus, I'm not talking about escape exactly. I'm talking about diversions, redirection and calling for help." He gave Adele an encouraging smile. "With the information you gave me, I think I know where we are."

Adele nodded slowly. "Where is that?"

It bothered him she would ask that question. She should want to escape, not to check his theories. He could lie. He could tell her the truth, or he could avoid the question. He looked at Vanessa.

She was glowering at Adele, but she wasn't saying anything snarky. Dylan figured that was progress.

"Do you have any way to keep time, Adele?" he asked, ignoring her question completely.

She frowned. "Why are you asking me that?"

I could ask the same of you. Dylan held up his watch. "So we can make sure we act at the same time. Unless they let you stay with us all night, and I'm not sure that's going to happen. So we should have a way to act in the same moment. If you can tell time, we can decide on one."

"I don't think there's anything in the room, but I'm not sure."

Dylan shook his head. By trying to play it confused and uncertain, she was only proving herself to be in on the whole kidnapping. Still, he'd keep pretending that he trusted her, for the sake of his real plan. No matter how he could hear Vanessa seething behind him.

"That's okay. We share a wall. I'll come up with a signal. Two knocks, pause, two more knocks. That's how you'll know it's time to act."

Adele frowned. "Act on what?"

"The plan."

"We don't need to involve everyone in the plan," Vanessa said through clenched teeth.

Dylan looked back at her and held her gaze, trying to get across that he knew what he was doing. She remained scowling and infuriated.

"We'll wait until the middle of the night. Vanessa's going to ask to go to the bathroom. I'll knock on our shared wall right before she does. You'll listen for them to move around, open our door, lead her to the bathroom. Then it'll be your turn. You'll start banging on the door asking to go to the bathroom. Now, one of them sleeps on a cot in some room off the kitchen. So we'll have one guard confused by two women needing to use the bathroom. In the meantime, I'll slip out of our room and put in a 911 call off the landline."

"The door will be locked," Adele pointed out. "Even if you get around that, they'll hear you talking to the 911 operator."

He ignored the part about getting around a locked door. She didn't need to know everything he was capable of. "I won't say anything. I'll dial and leave the phone off the hook. By the time the guard notices, the dispatcher will already be tracing the call and sending someone our way. I'm sure of it."

"Well…" Adele chewed on her bottom lip. "Maybe it could work. But what if they realize the phone is off the hook because one of us dialed 911? Do we really want to risk them hurting Vanessa?"

It was a question that might have struck fear into him a few minutes ago and given him another reason to believe Adele had nothing to do with this. But he'd seen the evidence. Thank God for pizza pockets.

"No. We don't want to risk *anyone* getting hurt, but the fact of the matter is Vanessa isn't getting the care she needs here. We need to get her out of here. As soon as possible."

"I am right here and fully capable of speaking for myself," Vanessa said, a warning quietness to her tone that he knew well enough. Soon she'd go nuclear. He almost wanted to see it.

Instead, he chose to ignore her, because her being furious worked into his plans well enough for now. "I can handle anything those guards can dish out."

"Yeah, I bet a bullet to the brain would be *real* easy to handle," Vanessa muttered.

"Vanessa has a point. They don't want to kill you, Dylan. You're the one with the rich family. Vanessa and I? They could kill us with no compunction. Why don't we just wait until the ransom is delivered? I'd feel better. They've threatened my family, you know."

Dylan kept himself relaxed even though he wanted to tense. "No, that's not information you chose to share."

She shook her head and closed her eyes. "I've

been so scared, so confused. Every step is a potential misstep and then my family is dead."

"I didn't realize you still had living family back in San Francisco." He'd chosen the city because he knew she wasn't from there. He wanted to see if he could catch her in another lie.

"We're not close, but I don't want them to die." Her voice trembled, and she produced more tears.

Dylan felt no softening this time. Adele was a believable actress, and he could think of enough scenarios where she might have been forced or threatened into cooperating. Blackmailed into helping rather than violently intimidated into keeping quiet like the tactic the goons had taken with him and Vanessa.

But her family *didn't* live in San Francisco. He might not know everything about her, but she'd never spoken of family. She had spoken of going to Seattle or Denver on occasion over holidays, and the assumption had been for family visits. She never mentioned San Francisco.

So it was the final nail in the Adele-has-always-been-against-us coffin.

Dylan couldn't let her know there were nails or coffins. Somehow, despite his rage and disappointment, he had to keep it all under wraps. And he had to make sure Vanessa didn't blow their cover either.

So he whirled to face her, giving her the most

murderous look he could manage while she sput-
tered and opened her mouth to certainly ask
Adele why she hadn't mentioned this earlier.

She gave him a murderous look right back, but
she didn't ask the question.

"Do you have a better plan, Adele?" Dylan
asked calmly.

"Yes. We wait until the ransom comes and they
let us go. They'll have to let us go."

"If you believe that, you're the dumbest human
on the face of the planet," Vanessa spat.

Adele straightened and glared right back at her.
"I beg your pardon."

"Do you?" Vanessa asked sweetly.

Adele returned the look. "I do beg your pardon.
Because getting mad at such a trashy whore who
doesn't even know the father of their baby is beneath me. So very, very far beneath me."

Vanessa straightened slowly, her hands clench-
ing into fists and giving Dylan no doubt she'd
throw a punch if given the chance. Dylan slid in
between the two angry women and focused on
Adele.

"Don't speak to her that way again, Adele."

"Hmm." She looked him up and down, cold,
calculating disdain in her gaze. "Did that hurt
your feelings?" she asked in a baby voice. "Because maybe she *does* know who the baby daddy

is, and maybe it's you?" She pretended to gasp. "What would *your* daddy say?"

He took a step toward her before he remembered he was playing a dangerous game here. If Adele was the mastermind, he had to play it cool. He could wring her neck, and what would it do? He still didn't know what she was after, and the men out there with guns could easily kill them without Adele to play her little games.

No matter how his temper boiled, he needed to understand this better. More importantly, he had to get Vanessa out of the crossfire range before he attempted anything.

"You're starting to sound jealous, Adele," Vanessa offered from behind Dylan's back.

God, she wasn't helping.

"Let's all calm down. We're tired. We're hungry. We're lashing out at each other at the worst possible moment. We need to band together." Or at least he needed Adele to believe they had.

Adele took in a deep breath and let it out. She nodded. "You're right, Dylan. Let's eat these awful things. We'll all feel better after."

Vanessa kept glaring, but she took a big bite of pizza pocket and chewed instead of arguing any more.

Chapter Fifteen

Vanessa hated to admit she felt better after eating. Too bad eating didn't cure the fact Adele was evil.

Was Dylan *really* this stupid? she wondered incredulously. She hadn't thought so. But he was going over the plan with Adele again as if he trusted her. As if he didn't see all the holes in her story.

Vanessa had stopped listening, stopped getting angry, because it was pointless. He was the dumbest man alive, and he'd deserve what he got when Adele turned on him and shot him through the heart.

Even in anger, that thought made her blood run cold, and she had to remind herself Adele clearly wanted Dylan alive for some reason. She'd had too many chances to kill him or have him killed.

It could be money. People had done less for money, but Vanessa didn't buy it. There was something bigger at stake here. If only she could figure out *what* before Dylan got his dumb self killed.

The door flung open to the sight of Eyeballs waving that butt of his gun around like it made him important. Vanessa barely resisted the urge to roll her eyes. He hadn't acted particularly quickly to use it as anything other than a battering ram against Dylan. Should they really be scared?

He grabbed Adele roughly by the arm. Adele whimpered and resisted, but Eyeballs squeezed hard enough to have Adele gasping.

Vanessa watched the whole thing as dispassionately as she might a play. Eyeballs could rough up Adele all he wanted, but unless he used even half the force against Adele that he'd used against Dylan, Vanessa wasn't buying this as anything more than a farce.

"Ransom time, and you're insurance, sweetheart." He pulled Adele toward the door. "I'd stop making all that noise before we start hurting that family of yours. We've got a man in San Fran ready to go."

"P-please. Don't…" Adele stopped struggling and let Eyeballs lead her out of the room, the door slamming shut and the lock clicking into place behind them.

"What a load of—"

Dylan held up a hand. Vanessa was tempted to punch it, but he put a finger to his lips. Quieting against her will, she watched him as he moved stealthily to the desk and began clicking keys on the computer.

He'd tried to get past the password protection earlier and failed, so she didn't know what he thought he was doing *now*. But after a few clicks where he seemed to just fiddle with the volume directly from the keyboard, he started to rummage through the desk.

He pulled out a piece of paper and a pen. Then he wrote in big fat letters: BUG.

She didn't understand what on earth he was doing. He'd seen a spider or a cockroach. Who gave a crap? "I'm supposed to be scared there's a b—"

His hand clamped over her mouth, sending the pen, paper and chair between them clattering to the ground. He gave her face a gentle squeeze, opening his eyes wider as if willing her to catch on. It took a minute, but then she finally got it.

Bug. Listening device. Had she fallen into some bizarre movie?

"They won't know what's coming," Dylan said cheerfully, slowly letting go of her face. "This 911 plan of mine is genius, and Adele helping us is huge."

Vanessa frowned at him. He didn't sound like himself, and wasn't he talking a little too loudly? But she couldn't exactly mount objections if they were being listened to.

He righted the chair and picked the pen and paper off the floor. He scribbled on it as he repeated the plan he'd made with Adele.

It was only now that there was a listening device and he was still going on about his 911 plan that Vanessa fully understood. He didn't trust Adele. He was setting her up.

She read the note he'd written.

I think the mic is in the computer. I didn't find anything earlier. Going to try to disable it.

Vanessa looked around the room. She tried not to think about the things Adele or her goons might have listened to or heard. Even though she hadn't revealed anything particularly telling, Dylan had. Because she'd made him.

A wave of regret washed over her. Whoever was listening knew who and what he was now. They wouldn't underestimate him anymore. They knew about the baby and that it was Dylan's. There were no secrets.

That was scary. Money could maybe buy silence but not forever, and Vanessa still didn't think this was about money.

"Dylan…" Except she couldn't talk because they were being listened to, and he kept trying to hack into the computer to turn off whatever was listening to them.

Vanessa glanced at the wires coming out of the desk and snaking their way to a power strip. She walked over, studied it. One of them had to power the computer, and without power to the computer...

She stepped on the thick main cord that hooked into the outlet, dislodging it. The computer went off with a *pop*. She looked up at Dylan and shrugged. "Oops."

He shook his head. "I was going for something a little less noticeable. If they notice the feed just die, they'll come fix it. Or put in a new listening device."

"I doubt they have backup listening devices. Besides, this looks like an accident—not that we knew they were listening. If they come and plug it back in, we know. And we can keep doing it as long as we need to."

Dylan looked around the room. "*If* that was the only listening device. I searched before, but Adele could have added one."

Exhaustion washed over her. *Another* listening device? How were they ever going to escape if someone could hear every word?

"They could be recording to play later too," Dylan said as if thinking it all through aloud. "So it might not be getting to them immediately, whatever we say. I certainly haven't heard them listening to anything when I've gone to get food, and you didn't hear anything when you went to the bathroom, did you?"

"No. But Adele's door was closed. *She* could be the listener."

Dylan nodded. "Adele wouldn't do that," Dylan said, but he made a big production of rolling his eyes and mouthing, *"She darn well would."*

Vanessa couldn't help but grin at him. He wasn't stupid after all. He was simply covering his tracks, throwing Adele off the scent. Thank God.

"Still, we need to be careful," he said. Then he wrote something down on a piece of paper and handed it to her.

I'm going to search the room one more time with a better idea of what I'm looking for.

It felt like he took hours. He left no stone unturned. She almost nodded off on the chair, but then he made her get up so he could search the chair.

"You're tired," he said as he poked at folds in the fabric and pushed on the cushion—presumably looking for something hard inside.

"Exhausted," she returned.

"I'm tempted to demand some kind of bed, but

if they're off pretending to collect ransom, maybe the best thing is to keep a low profile. I'm about ninety-nine percent sure there's no other listening device, and the fact they haven't busted in to turn the computer back on or tell us we'll never call 911 makes me think they're just recording, not listening in. So we'll take a few hours to sleep."

"I want to go home." She did, desperately. So much so her eyes were starting to sting.

He crossed the room to her, sliding his hands over her shoulders. That touch, the simple *care* in his gaze, just about had the tears spilling over.

"I know. I know. I'm going to get you home." A promise. A vow.

She hated that tears spilled, that something like a sob escaped her throat. But instead of being horrified or letting her wiggle out of his grasp, he simply pulled her to him. He held her there, putting gentle pressure on her head until she rested it on his shoulder.

He didn't say anything—nothing to try to make her feel better or stop crying. He simply let her cry there on his shoulder, rubbing his hand up and down her spine.

So she wept. In a way she'd never, *ever* done in someone's presence before. She let it all out, like she was alone in the shower or something. But she wasn't alone. She had Dylan. And he was holding her like he always would.

She really had to get ahold of herself. Crying was ridiculous, but thinking about *always* was the height of ridiculousness. She pulled away from his grasp, wiping at her face with the palms of her hands.

"I'm—"

"I know you're not about to apologize for crying after you've been kidnapped and had a major head injury that caused temporary memory loss, all while pregnant I might add. Because that kind of apology would just be stupid."

She sniffled, glaring at him, which she assumed had been his intent. Get her back up and a little irritated with him so she wouldn't start blubbering again.

"You need to rest up," he said gently. "We have to see what comes of this ransom thing." He looked at his clock. "I want the second guard fast asleep before…" He trailed off, still worried about the prospect of being recorded or heard.

"They won't be able to hear a sound if they're still recording," she whispered. She was too tired to wait around for him to write notes and then keep her eyes open to read them.

"We're not going to call 911. Well, we are, but we're going to escape in the process. We will not spend another twenty-four hours in this cabin, I promise you that."

"You really think we can escape?" she whispered.

"I'm going to get you home. It's a promise."

She frowned at the way he worded that—so it was about her, not them—but he walked away and started chattering on about finding a makeshift bed.

IT WOULDN'T BE a comfortable nap, but it was sleep and that's what was important. Dylan had stacked two rugs on top of each other, tilted the chair on the ground so the headrest could act as a pillow of sorts and found a drop cloth in the closet that could act like a blanket.

She watched him the whole time he worked, wary and speculative.

He ignored all those things in her because the quiet worked. He needed to slightly reformulate his plan, and being able to do it without her questioning or arguing was easier. "Here. It's not luxury, but it'll do." He gestured her toward the makeshift bed.

"You think I'm used to luxury?" She stood where she was, eyebrow raised at the sad attempt at a bed. "Where are you going to sleep?"

He gestured toward the door. "Against it. That way, if they come in, we're ready. I can sleep against anything." He forced himself to smile. "All that army training."

She walked over to the pretend bed and scrunched

up her face, but eventually lowered herself into it. She leaned her head against the headrest acting as a pillow, and then studied him.

He didn't mind being studied by her. Didn't mind *her*. Life had changed in a blink. He was still trying to wade through what that meant, but he couldn't get a handle on it until he knew she was safe.

Everything else could be dealt with once that happened.

Eventually, Vanessa patted the spot next to her. "Come here. There's room."

It was amazing how much he wanted to—a physical need he had to beat back. "Better to be ready." Sleep on the door so they couldn't be taken unawares.

"Come here, I said. Aren't soldiers supposed to follow orders?"

There was enough steel in her tone to have him smiling. "I haven't been a soldier in years."

"You've done an impressive impression of one these past two days. Now, do as Captain Vanessa says and get over here."

"Captain, huh?"

"You're right. I'm really better suited to general."

He chuckled, and really, what was the point in resisting? He'd protect her whether he slept next to her or against the door. Besides, he probably wouldn't sleep at all. Though getting an hour or two would keep him sharp, and he was pretty good at sleeping when he needed to, he'd never been in the position before of protecting so much that was valuable to him.

On a sigh, he crawled into the fake bed, facing her. They were close enough he could feel her warmth, count each faint freckle on her nose and the long inky lashes of her eyes.

"When did you figure it out?" she whispered.

He didn't have to ask her what she meant. "I've been suspicious the whole time, but Adele's a good actress and I… It's hard to believe someone you've trusted is willing to hurt you."

Something in her expression shuttered. "Not for everyone."

He didn't know much about her childhood, but he knew enough. The Carson generation that had raised the current one was full of hard men, mean men. Violent men. He'd used that as an excuse to hate all Carsons, but the truth was…

Hell, Grady was an okay guy. Dylan had never had a problem with Noah. Ty…well, sometimes he'd like to knock that guy's block off, but none of them were like their fathers.

"No. I guess you're right." Unable to stop himself, he reached out and brushed some hair off her face. "But no one ever gave you a reason to trust them not to hurt you."

She shrugged jerkily. "Grady. Noah and Ty."

"That's different. Believe me. When it's just kids it's different. You need an adult who has your back. You guys never had that."

"You softening to Carsons, Delaney?"

"I'm going to be a father to half of one. I figure I better."

She held his gaze, and he saw everything he felt reflected there. Fear. Hope. Care.

"So, what sealed the deal? Regarding Adele?" she asked, her voice thick. He told himself it was exhaustion, but part of him wondered if it was emotion.

"When they took me to the kitchen to make the pizza pockets, I was trying to look around. See out windows, anything that might give me an idea where we are, and the door to the room she'd been in was open. There were two perfectly normal-sized windows. A computer. She's running the show, and the guys she hired to be the muscle don't have two brain cells between them."

Vanessa blew out a breath, sliding closer to him. Like this was their normal life. Nightly conversations in bed together where they weren't kidnapped and trying to sleep on the floor with office materials as bedding.

"I think it centers on the bank and on her job. When you were out there, she was getting so angry with me. I kept poking at the bank, at your dad. It's something about that."

"Well, the bank is an endless source of money."

Vanessa shook her head. "It isn't about money." He noted she kept her voice at the lowest whisper yet. "I know it's not about money. You have to find the connection to the bank."

"She's off getting the ransom."

"It's a ploy or a lie." Her lips all but brushed his ear, and it was the absolute wrong time to feel the wave of lust and want coming over him.

"What's a bigger motivation than money?" he asked, trying to keep his brain focused on the task at hand instead of being distracted by the way she shifted closer, so their bodies pressed together.

"I'm not sure I can come up with anything," she said, rubbing her cheek against his jaw. "If you've got money, which it seems like she does, at least enough to get by on, why would you go through all this for more? It has to be something else. Too bad we can't ask your dad."

Dylan smirked. "He'd always take more."

"Sure. We all would, but this is about what you'd risk. Why risk everything for money if you've got it?"

"Secret gambling habit? A family member's bills for an illness? This cabin?"

"No. It doesn't add up. This is something personal."

"Or she's mentally unstable. Also a thought we should consider."

Vanessa closed her eyes. "I'm so tired of considering."

He brushed his mouth over her temple, wanting to soothe both her and himself. He wanted them out of this too. Wanted her checked out and safe and sound at home.

Home. Something they'd have to talk about, because he'd be damned if she raised their baby over her greasy deathtrap of a mechanic shop, and he had no doubt she'd fight tooth and nail to make sure their baby wasn't raised anywhere near Delaney property.

He rested his cheek on top of her head and held her close. They had all sorts of challenges ahead. The predicament they were currently in. The baby. But something in this quiet moment resisted all need to figure it out. He wanted to breathe, and he wanted peace.

Vanessa sighed against his neck. "I know it doesn't make any sense," she whispered, and this time he didn't think it was because of the potential of being overheard. "But we fit."

"Yeah, we do."

She pressed her mouth to his neck and then his jaw, sliding her body sinuously against his.

"Well." He had to clear his throat since it was suddenly dry as dust.

This time her mouth touched his, light and teasing, and then she nipped, causing his grip on her to tighten, just like the rest of his body.

"And for about five minutes," she murmured, right against his lips, "I'd like to pretend that's the most important thing in my life."

"Five minutes?" he scoffed. "Really?"

She chuckled against his mouth, maneuvering herself on top of him. "I don't need more."

Dylan slid his hands down her sides, enjoying the sweet pleasure of the friction between their bodies, even with clothes on. "I do."

She flashed him a grin. "Wanna bet?"

Chapter Sixteen

Even though bets were what had gotten them into this mess—something she remembered around the time her clothes were quickly being removed from her body—this one felt right. He felt right. They fit together.

Maybe when they were back in the real world, she'd have to deal with that a little more head-on, but the real world wasn't here.

She took a moment to trace her finger over the small tattoo on his chest. She recognized it as the Delaney brand. It touched her. She had a quite a few tattoos herself, and some had heavy meanings, but she'd never branded herself with her family's legacy. It seemed both noble and a little sad that Dylan of all people had.

But she couldn't hold on to sad when Dylan slid into her. There was no world at the moment except them together. It was peace, and it was bliss. It didn't matter he was a Delaney, only that his body moving with hers felt perfectly right.

"Van," he murmured as she arched against him. He spoke her shortened name as if it was a precious, solemn prayer. He touched her like she was his to care for, and everything in her shimmered with a life she didn't know how to control or put her own impenetrable shell over.

"I want you. Us." *Us.* She wanted there to be a *them*. Her brain couldn't wrap itself around that simple fact, but her heart had already made the leap. Maybe even before this whole mess. Maybe on that fuzzy night they'd conceived a child together.

She sighed into her release, holding him close as he found his own. When she drifted off, the sleep was deep, long and perfectly happy.

When she woke up—she wasn't sure how much later—she was somehow dressed and curled up in the makeshift bed Dylan had made. He was curled up behind her, arms wrapped protectively around her stomach.

She closed her eyes again, wanting to sink into this feeling of utter safety, no matter how uncomfortable the bed was.

But Dylan shifted, tightening then loosening his grip. She could feel him coming awake next to her, and the real world crashing back into them. She could tell his brain immediately clicked into gear, working out what the next step was.

Fear washed through her. Bone-deep fear that she'd lose him somehow.

"Are you sure it isn't safe to just wait? Surely someone's looking for you." A tension she didn't know how to label crept into her shoulders, and suddenly she felt...insignificant. "Do you think anyone knows where I am? I'm sure all of Wyoming has been rallied to look for Dylan Delaney, but does anyone know I'm a part of this?"

"Your car was in the bank parking lot. I'd wager there's an army of Carsons convinced *I* kidnapped *you*. They're probably roaming the mountains looking to take me down."

Vanessa laughed, snuggling into him. It was a nice feeling. Definitely new. She'd never considered herself a cuddler or a hugger. She got to sneak some cuddle time in with Noah and Addie's kid, but he was quickly turning into a toddler who squirmed and wiggled away.

She slid a hand over her stomach, and Dylan did the same. Their fingers brushed, both palms resting over the life they'd made.

"I know it's not the time to discuss it since we have to survive this all first, but how are we going to do this?" she asked, swamped with so much emotion she had to get it all out lest she fall apart again.

"I notice you've switched to *we* instead of cutting me out completely."

She turned in the circle of his arms to face him. "I guess you saving my butt a few times here and there during this whole ordeal softened me up."

"It's my fault you're even—"

"No, it's Adele's fault." Vanessa sat up and rubbed her eyes. There was a low-level queasiness in her stomach, but it wasn't as bad as usual. They could and probably should talk about not cutting him out of the future, but the reminder of Adele brought back the fact they had to survive first.

"Do you think she's back?"

Dylan pointed up to the windows. "It's still dark, but you can see dawn creeping in. She'd have to be back, wouldn't she?"

"There's one way to find out." Vanessa pushed to her feet and started for the door.

"Van—"

She looked over her shoulder at Dylan and winked. "Sorry, Charlie, pregnant women gotta pee and you aren't invited." She started pounding on the door even as he glared at her grumpily.

It took longer than usual for No-Neck to answer the door. He looked a little rumpled, like he'd been asleep. Vanessa raised an eyebrow at him.

"Go to the bathroom. Try anything funny and I'll shoot." He led her out but didn't grab her by both arms. Before she even got to the bathroom, he let her go and trudged over to the kitchen area and began fumbling with a coffee machine.

Vanessa walked slowly toward the bathroom door, looking around the living room for signs of Adele. She didn't see the evil mastermind, but she did note that where there had once been a land-line phone, there was now an empty end table.

Evil witch.

"Get on with it," No-Neck grumbled, waving his coffee mug at her.

She did as she was told and went to the bathroom. Since No-Neck was preoccupied, she took her time to paw through the cabinet under the sink, but there was nothing weapon worthy or helpful.

On a grunt of frustration she stood, just as No-Neck jerked the door open.

"Hey!" Vanessa protested.

"You're taking too long."

She sailed out of the bathroom past him. "You're cheery in the morning."

He gave her a shove, and only quick reflexes kept her stomach from slamming into the back of the couch. She turned to glare at him, but he was too busy gulping down his coffee and wincing, presumably at the scalding heat.

"Where's your buddy?" she asked.

"None of your business. You want another

shove or you going to go back to your room on your own two feet?"

It was *so* tempting to say something snarky in return. She briefly considered smacking the coffee mug so that it spilled on him. It would be enough of a distraction to…

What? Get to the door and be shot in the back?

Scowling, she sailed back to the room. She was going to grab the door herself, see if she could con him into forgetting to lock it behind her, but No-Neck was there in a flash, opening the door and pushing her inside.

She whirled and glared at him, which was good because she didn't look at Dylan standing right next to the door, pressed to the wall so he was out of sight from No-Neck.

As No-Neck grinned snidely at her scowl, he pulled the door closed. While he did it, Dylan soundlessly slipped something between the door and the frame.

"What—"

Dylan held a finger to his lips and shook his head. He led her over to the far corner of the room and then leaned down to whisper in her ear.

"Tape on the lock. Found some when I was looking for the bug. Not sure I got it on like I needed to, or that it's strong enough to keep the lock from engaging, but it was worth a shot." He shrugged. "We'll test it later. See anything out there? Adele?"

"Just No-Neck, but the phone that was on that table is gone."

Dylan didn't panic or frown or do anything she expected. He grinned.

"Why are you *happy* about that? It means we can't call 911! Our plan is shot to hell."

"Babe, that was never the plan."

She scowled at him. "Take your *babe* and shove it where the sun don't shine."

He grinned more broadly. "*And* it proves Adele is behind this."

"Yeah, because the giant window you saw in her room didn't," she returned sarcastically. "So, now what?"

"Now—" he took her by the shoulders, holding her gaze "—we plan *our* escape."

LAUREL COULD HAVE used a jumbo coffee. Instead she had to settle for water, because she'd inhaled her caffeine intake for the day by approximately 7 a.m. Now it was well after noon and she had been summoned to the Delaney Ranch to deal with her father.

She'd left Hart poring over the bank records they'd finally managed to get under subpoena. Still no cell phone ping to help them.

With a headache drumming at her temples, she knocked on the door and then stepped inside.

"Dad?"

"He's upstairs." Jen stepped out from the kitchen, where she usually was if she was home. "No word?"

Laurel shook her head and exchanged a quick hug with her sister. "State is setting up for a potential ransom drop-off, but they're having trouble getting details from the kidnapper. Apparently she's fallen off the face of the planet after her demand for money."

"Her?" Jen asked with a raised eyebrow.

"That's my theory." Which, much as she loved her sister, Laurel wasn't going to share more of. "Do you have any idea why Dad wanted me to come by?"

Jen shook her head. "He's been holed up in his office since he woke up. He wouldn't even talk to Cam when he stopped in." Jen looked up at the ceiling, worry lines creasing her forehead.

"Did Cam go out looking again?"

Jen nodded, wringing her hands. "I wish there was something *I* could do."

"Watching Dad is what I need you to do, okay? It's not fun, I know, but it's important."

"He's a mess."

Laurel nodded. "I'll head up. Thanks for staying with him while we work on this."

"You know you don't have to thank me."

"Yeah." Laurel thought briefly of telling Jen about the baby. She'd agreed with Grady not to tell anyone until she was further along, but Jen was her sister and her closest friend. Not to mention she'd had to tell Hart. "Listen…" Laurel chewed on her bottom lip. "You didn't see anything going on between Vanessa and Dylan at my wedding, did you?"

"Dylan and Vanessa?" Jen laughed. Hard. "You mean other than pure, unfiltered hatred?"

"Yeah, other than that."

"No. I mean… I don't remember really seeing them that much." Jen got a weird look on her face and then shook it away. "Do you really think they're together?"

"In more ways than one."

"That can't be," Jen said, surprisingly adamant.

"All evidence points to—"

"I don't care what all evidence points to. You and Grady are bad enough but Dyl…" She trailed off, squeezing her eyes shut. "I don't mean it like *that*."

"Yes, you do," Laurel said. Normally, it didn't bother her. Her family was set in their feuding ways, except Cam. She'd accepted that, moved on. But with being pregnant and Dylan missing, it stirred up…

Well, feelings she didn't have time for. "I'll be

back," she murmured, heading away from Jen and her apologies and toward the stairs. She trudged up them, tired and dreading any discussion with her father while Dylan remained missing.

She knocked on the closed office door, only stepping inside once her father said come in.

"You wanted to see me."

"I've been sent another correspondence."

"What? And you didn't forward—"

"It was on the porch this morning," he interrupted, nodding to a manila envelope on the desk.

"How long ago?"

Dad shrugged.

"Dad. What's wrong with you? Why didn't you call me sooner? Why didn't you tell me you found a lead?" She was already pulling her latex gloves out of the pouch on her utility belt as Dad pulled a photograph out of the envelope. "You've got your prints on it."

It was grainy, but very clearly showed Dylan and Vanessa in a room that seemed to be a kind of office, arms around each other.

"Put it down. We could get prints off of it. We could—"

"Do you see what is happening in this picture?" Dad demanded, shoving it into her face. "And it isn't just this picture. The envelope is full of evidence my son has been lying to me for years. About everything. His education. His entire *life*, and now there's some nonsense about that *Carson* woman being pregnant and…" The rage on his face went cold. "You don't seem surprised."

"I knew Vanessa was pregnant as part of the course of the investigation," Laurel returned coolly. "Whatever other lies you're referring to, I'm in the dark on."

"And the baby being Dylan's?" Dad all but spat.

"It was a theory."

"How could you both be so—"

"No. No. We're not doing this. We're trying to find Dylan and Vanessa. You… How could you jeopardize them this way? You should have called me the second you got these. You never should have… How can you do this? All over something so insignificant."

"Insignificant? If he dared impregnate that scum—"

"What is wrong with you?" she demanded, temper bubbling over. "Dylan could be *dead* because of you."

He paled at that, but he still grasped the picture. "He's dead to me if this is true."

Laurel reached out and slapped him across the face before she'd even thought the action through. She expected regret to wash through her, but there was none. Dylan was in danger and an innocent bystander—a pregnant woman—was in trouble, and all Dad cared about was the family reputation.

"You're sick and twisted," she managed, though her voice cracked along with her heart. She ignored the tears of hot rage that spilled over. "Your son is in grave danger and all you care about is a *name*. A dusty old feud. You still talk to me and Cam, but this is somehow unforgivable?"

"You and Cam are not creating *children* with those mongrels. It goes against all our history. It goes against the very nature of Bent, Laurel. Carsons and Delaneys were not meant to be. Have you noticed what hell has gone on since you started your thing with Grady?"

She ignored the last part. She wouldn't let him put this on her. She wouldn't let him put this on *love*. "I am. I *am* creating children."

"I know you think that, but Carson will show his true colors before you—"

"No, Dad. I'm pregnant."

The picture in his hands fluttered to the ground and he sat with an audible thump.

"Your future grandchildren are all part Carson thus far. I hope they all will be. And I hope to God you get it through your head that's something to be proud of."

Laurel refused to look at her father. She had a job to do. She pulled on the gloves so she could touch the pictures and envelope without adding her own prints.

"I don't know where I went so wrong with you children," Dad said, his voice faint and thready. "I taught you what was right, and this is how you've all repaid me."

"You did. You taught us the difference between right and wrong, justice and injustice." Hadn't he? Hadn't his four children grown up to be upstanding members of the community because he'd instilled in them a responsibility to do what was right? But the past year had shown her over and over again that her father didn't know what right was. "I don't know what happened to you that you can't see it."

"You're cursing us," Dad said, his voice sounding brittle and desperate.

Through this whole ordeal she'd wondered, no matter how stupid or utterly fantastical, if she hadn't cursed the town by loving the wrong man.

Except the man she loved was not wrong, in any way, shape or form.

"No. The curse all these years is this." She gestured at him. "This pointless, relentless hate. It's what you've all gotten wrong for over a hundred years. Hate doesn't solve a damn thing. It never has. It never will." She looked at her father, unbearably hurt. "But love will."

She'd believed in right and wrong, truth and

justice, her entire life. She'd built her career and her soul on that very foundation, but the truth of the matter was that underneath that foundation was a base of love.

"I hope you change your mind in time to be the grandfather our children deserve." Because with love came hope and, hopefully at some point, forgiveness. "Now, while I'm busting my butt to get my brother home safe and sound, I hope you'll take some time to think about what you want to be the center of your life. Some stupid, pointless feud or your family."

She took the picture and the envelope and left her father silent and brooding. She sucked in a breath and let it out, compartmentalizing the hurt so she could do her job.

She left without saying goodbye to Jen, got to her car and bagged up the evidence. As she was backing up, her cell rang. She answered.

"I think I found it," Hart said, sounding breathless. "I called backup. We're heading out now."

"Address," Laurel barked.

"No way, Laurel."

"It's my brother."

"Exactly. I've got the manpower to handle it myself, and you've got the manpower to sit at a desk and wait."

She hated that he was right. She couldn't risk herself and her baby. She had to believe Hart could handle it. Which burned—enough that she said something she thought she'd never say.

"Fine, but I'm sending in my own backup."

"Laurel, I don't need Carsons."

"But you're going to get them." She always played by the rules, but if she couldn't be there to save her brother, she'd darn well send in a bunch of guys who would break every rule possible to save the people they and she loved.

Chapter Seventeen

Dylan could wait with the best of them. He was a trained sniper. He could sit in one uncomfortable position for hours on end, gun at the ready. It had been his life for a couple years, and his capacity for patience and control hadn't just evaporated the moment he'd reentered civilian life.

But waiting with an impatient pregnant woman who couldn't sit still to save her life was driving him insane.

"Babe, you've got to sit."

She glared at him. "This whole *babe* crap is getting real old, real fast."

He grinned. "Okay, no babe. Honey, you've got to sit."

She crossed her arms over her chest. "Real cute."

"I know." But because he knew her glares and irritation were really nerves, he crossed to her and put his hands on her shoulders. He gave them a reassuring squeeze. "Waiting is the hardest part, but it's the most crucial. Timing is everything."

"We don't even know if the tape worked. Shouldn't we check?"

"We have to wait."

She groaned and tried to wiggle away from his grasp, but he only wound his arms around her waist and pulled her close, dropping a kiss to her neck. "I could distract you," he murmured, enjoying the way her resistance slowly melted into him.

But she didn't relax fully, and she kept her palms on his chest for distance. She looked up at him, some attempt at skepticism keeping her mouth from curving, but her eyes gave her away. He was tempted to tell her how easily they did, but he figured she'd only make sure they didn't anymore.

The slight humor there faded though, and she grew serious. "If this works—"

"*When* this works," he corrected.

She blew out a breath. "Fine. *When* this works, and we're back home, we sure have a whole hell of a lot to figure out."

"Maybe. Maybe that's all just details. Bottom line, when we're back home, you and I do everything to build the best life for our baby."

Her eyebrows drew together. "We'll never agree on the best life."

Dylan shrugged. "I think you'll be surprised

by how much we'll agree on. But, first and foremost, we need to get out of here. So let's go over it one more time."

She groaned again, and again he held tight when she tried to push him away. "Lay it out for me," he instructed.

She glared at him, but did as she was told. "We wait until four, which is when they start their evening switch-off. No-Neck takes his little nap, and Eyeballs makes his dinner. We see if the tape worked, and if it did, we slip out. Me first. Then you."

"And if Eyeballs sees, or Adele pops up from wherever she's hiding?"

"I say I had to go to the bathroom and they forgot to lock the door. If pressed, I admit you picked the lock and forced me as a sacrifice to try to leave. If they start moving for your door, I scream and say I saw a spider. You'll create a diversion, and I'll run." She looked up at him, and this time he was pretty sure she let him see all the emotion on her face on purpose. "I don't like that part, Dylan."

He rested his forehead on hers. "I know, but we have to get you out of here, and the bottom line is if you're not in firing range, I can take out those two nimrods."

He wasn't scared of sacrificing himself. The way he saw it, unless there was some big surprise waiting for him, he had an 85 percent chance of survival. As long as she didn't try to interfere.

Which meant he had to make sure she didn't. No easy feat when the woman in question was as contrary as they came. But they had more at stake than each other.

"Van, it only works if you run no matter what. No looking back. No trying to save me. It only works if you're off like a shot and leave me to deal with them."

"Dylan—"

"You have to run. You have more than just yourself to think of. Besides, I can handle myself."

"I'm not just going to—"

"Promise me."

"I want it to be clear the only damn reason I'm doing this is because I'm pregnant, and I promised myself a long time ago I would do whatever it took to be the mother my mom wasn't and put my baby first. That's it. The *only* reason I'm letting you do this. Carsons don't run. They protect what's theirs."

He smiled. "So protect what's yours."

"You're both mine," she said fiercely. And she didn't take it back or look away. She held his gaze, serious and determined.

It rippled through him, all that it meant, all that he felt. The thing was, feelings were dangerous.

They led to mistakes, and he couldn't afford any. His first instinct was to compartmentalize, put them away for later.

But he needed Vanessa to understand, to do what he asked. Which meant he'd use those feelings, *then* put them away.

He pulled back enough to frame her face with his hands, ignoring the fact they might have trembled just a little. "I never thought I'd fall in love with a Carson."

He ignored her sharp intake of breath and kept talking.

"Or during a kidnapping. Or after I'd already gotten someone pregnant. But maybe it's fitting, all in all."

He felt the tremble in her own body, watched the way she swallowed. Hard. "Well," she managed on a shaky breath. "I'm pretty sure even a week ago I would have told you I'd rather drink bleach than fall in love with a Delaney."

"Lovely."

"But I think I felt that way because…well, not because I hate Delaneys."

"You sure about that?"

"I hate your dad. And sometimes I just want to punch Cam in his perfect face for no real reason. I've never hated Laurel. I…" Her shoulders slumped and she pressed a few fingers right under the bump on her head that was slowly lessening in swelling. "We were friends. We didn't stop being friends because I *hated* her. It's complicated. And with Jen I'm mostly just ambivalent."

"That's my father and my siblings, but so far nothing about me."

She took a deep breath and pushed it out. "There's been something between us for a long time."

"Yeah, there has." Something undeniable in so many ways.

"I wanted it to be hate, but maybe it never really was."

He pushed some hair behind her ears. So many pieces inside of him that he'd hidden or locked away or tensed eased suddenly. "Yeah, maybe."

"Maybe that's always what's gone wrong. People have seen hate where there was really love and…well, anyway. I guess what I'm saying is I love you too, and I'd say I don't know why, but I know. You're good, and underneath all that polish you're as tough as any Carson. You care and I… This isn't some goodbye, is it? Because I'm not letting you out of this. We're riding back into Bent together. Screw their curse."

He smiled, because it was so her. Because he hoped they could make that happen. "No goodbyes. I just want you to know what's at stake. So you can promise me you'll run. You'll run and you'll protect that baby. And if you get a chance to call your brother and cousins to help me out here, I wouldn't say no."

"You don't want me to call Laurel and the police?"

He eyed the door, considered that. "I'd take both."

She took his wrist, tilted the watch to her gaze. "Looks like it's show time."

But he didn't release her. He held her tighter. "Promise me."

She shook her head, but she looked him in the eye. "I promise. I'll run. And I'll trust you to fight your own battle." She took his hand and placed it over her stomach. "But remember what you're fighting for."

He nodded. Kissed her once, hard, and then put it all away. Tied it up and shoved it out of his brain. It was a shame he couldn't, just for the next few minutes, shove it out of his heart.

He released her and a breath. "All right. Here goes nothing." He moved to the door. With care and patience he could all but feel made her bristle, Dylan twisted the knob. It gave, slowly and silently, and he ignored the excitement pounding in his chest.

He twisted the full way, then pulled. The door gave for a second, but then caught. He wanted to swear, but instead he kept his mind clear, calm.

"I need something to wiggle in here. Something thin enough to fit through the door crack. Like a credit card or a hair pin. Find me something." He held the doorknob turned all the way, ignoring the impulse to jerk the door open. They needed quiet.

And a metric ton of luck.

Vanessa hopped to work, pawing through the things on the desk. She found a spiral notebook and ripped the cover off. She held it up to him and when he nodded, she ripped it in half.

"Smaller," he instructed. She ripped it again and again until it was the size he wanted. She handed it to him, and he slid it into the space between door and frame. He wiggled the light but firm cardboard cover against the lock partially engaged by the tape.

It worked. He eased the door open.

The living room was empty, and as suspected, he could hear someone moving around in the kitchen.

He motioned Vanessa out, and she followed the plan, moving quickly and quietly to the front door while Dylan scanned the room for weapons he could use if they were caught. There wasn't really anything, but he trusted his fists—and his wits.

He didn't dare watch Vanessa since he had to observe the opening to the kitchen to make sure no one popped out. At one point he heard the faintest squeak of the front door and winced, then readied his body to attack.

But no one came.

Heart thudding with too much hope to contain, Dylan began to back away from the living-room opening and toward the door. It couldn't be this easy. It couldn't be, and yet…

He made it to the door where Vanessa was poised in the opening she'd made, just big enough for her body. He nodded to her, then took the doorknob from her grasp.

He'd need to make the opening a little bigger to fit himself out. As he did, the door squeaked. It was faint, but he knew they would hear it.

Dylan gave himself one precious moment to look Vanessa in the eye. "Run." He gave her a little shove, shut the door and prayed to God she listened.

VANESSA RAN.

Tears threatened, some mix of anger and fear. What an idiot he was, shoving the door closed so he had to handle it all himself. That was not going to fly if they got back to Bent and got to plan their lives together.

"When. *When* we get back to Bent," she whispered to herself, running for the trees. Dylan had instructed her to run there first. Deep enough she couldn't see the house. Then she was supposed to stop and listen. If she didn't hear anyone coming after her, she was supposed to slowly inch her way back, using as much cover as she could, then follow the road back down the mountain.

If anyone came out of the cabin, she was supposed to run as deep into the woods as she could, and trust he'd be able to find her once he took care of everyone.

It was a desperate, stupid plan and she wanted to punch herself in the face for ever listening to it. But she stopped, deep enough she could just barely make out the faint color of the cabin far off in the distance through the trees.

They didn't come after her. For as long as that was true, Dylan was alive.

Unless you don't matter and they only wanted him.

She choked on a sob, but she got out of the crouch and slid slowly and carefully between trees, getting closer and closer to the tree line until she could make out the road.

She noticed there were two cars in front of the cabin and tried not to let that worry her. Nothing could worry her except getting the baby inside of her back to safety.

Another sob escaped her mouth, but she bit her lip to keep the rest in. She kept behind trees, moving forward quietly and carefully through the woods parallel to the road.

After a while, the sobs stopped and tears dried, and all she had was a grim determination to keep walking no matter how badly her feet hurt or her head throbbed.

When she reached a fork in the road, tears threatened again. She didn't know where she was. Should she try to cross the road and follow the opposite path? Or follow this one under cover? What if it wrapped back up into the mountain? What if she crossed the road and someone started shooting?

She couldn't take the risk of stepping into the open. One way or another, either fork would lead her somewhere eventually. She stayed on the fork that allowed her to keep in the tree line and trudged on.

On and on, until she had to stop and lean against trees for support every few minutes. Her head was spinning and her mouth was too dry. She was wrung out and dead on her feet.

But Dylan was back there somewhere fighting two armed men, and she had to save him. Somehow, she had to save him. She needed to get to a town, to a—

She stopped abruptly at the sight of a car parked on the other side of the road. Someone was leaning against the hood.

Vanessa held very still, squinting through the trees. It was a tan car, with some kind of logo on the side. A logo she knew. And the person in baggy clothes and a puffy coat leaning against the hood was—

"Laurel." When Laurel didn't move, Vanessa realized she hadn't really said it. She'd gasped it, afraid it was a mirage. But as she weakly stepped forward, the police cruiser didn't waver and disappear. Laurel's serious profile didn't morph or change. She wasn't hallucinating. She wasn't.

Vanessa kept moving for open air and the road, still waiting for the image to disappear. "Laurel," she said as she stumbled through the tree line.

Laurel's head whipped around, and it didn't escape Vanessa's notice that her hand went straight for her weapon, though she didn't draw.

"Oh, my God. Oh, my God." Laurel dropped her hand from the weapon and immediately rushed across the road.

She was at Vanessa's side in a flash, and for a moment all Vanessa could think to do was hug her and sob. It was real. Laurel was here, and Dylan had gotten her out. She leaned against Laurel's shorter frame, squeezed her as tight as the strength she had in her body allowed and sobbed.

Laurel pulled away, though she held Vanessa upright, which was about the only thing doing the job at the moment.

"Dylan," Laurel said, eyes searching and scared. "Where's Dylan?"

"He's still there. He needs help." Vanessa swallowed, summoning her strength. "He's back there. He's back there. Come on." She grabbed Laurel's arm. "You've got a gun and a badge. I'll lead you."

But Laurel didn't budge. "We're not going back there, Van."

Panic and fear skittered up her spine. "What the hell is wrong with you? He's back there fighting off two goons with guns and a crazy woman. You have to get to him."

Laurel closed her eyes as if against some great pain, but still she didn't let Vanessa pull her toward the trees. "My men are handling it."

"Your *men*? Since when do you let a bunch of Podunk deputies save your flesh and blood?"

"Vanessa. Calm down." Laurel used her free arm to pull Vanessa's hand into hers. "Are you all right? I should call you an ambulance. Come on." She started leading Vanessa a few steps toward the police cruiser before Vanessa skidded them to a halt.

"No! I'm not going anywhere until Dylan is safe and sound. You have to find him, Laurel. You have to save him."

Laurel nodded. "We are. They're surrounding the cabin as we speak."

"It should be you."

Again, Laurel looked incredibly pained, but

her voice was level and calm. Her cop voice. "It can't be me. For the same reason Dylan got you out of there."

"You…" It took a moment, or a few, to connect all the dots. Laurel knew. And she was… "You know."

"We had to search your place. Hold on." She lifted the radio on her uniform to her mouth and started using codes and police blabber to explain Vanessa was with her. "Two men with guns, and one woman? Adele Oscar?"

"Yes. You knew?"

Laurel led her to the passenger's side of the cruiser and opened the door. "We figured some things out." Gently, Laurel nudged her into the passenger seat. "So, it's true. Dylan is…"

"The father of my baby? Yes. I surely hope Grady is the father of yours."

Laurel gave her a baleful look, then gently closed the door. She marched around the front of the car, then took her seat behind the steering wheel.

"We can't just sit here."

"We have to." Laurel shook her head. "You have to know it's killing me too, but…sometimes a woman has to make a sacrifice a man never has to make. We're making it. If it makes you feel any better, I gave Grady the address. It's not just my deputies up there."

Vanessa relaxed into the seat. "Thank God. Someone with some brains." And all the people she loved were in danger. "There has to be something I can do," she whispered to Laurel.

"There is. You're going to tell me everything you know about who's in there, what the layout is and what dumb plan got you out and is no doubt about to get my brother hurt, while I drive you to the hospital to get checked out."

Vanessa's eyes flew open and she reached out and grabbed Laurel's arm. "I'm not going anywhere until Dylan's out. I'll tell you everything right here, and once they get him out safe and sound we go up there. He's hurt too. Not bad, or at least it wasn't bad before. I'm not going anywhere without him."

"You love him," Laurel murmured. There was shock in her voice, but not censure. Then again, of all the Delaneys to censure it, Laurel didn't have a leg to stand on.

"Maybe I always did," she muttered.

Laurel smiled gently, taking Vanessa's hand off her arm and then squeezing it and interlocking their fingers. "I know the feeling. Now, tell me everything."

So Vanessa did.

Chapter Eighteen

The fight was a brutal marathon, but Dylan was still alive. He figured that was something. Now, if he could just get his hands on one of their guns, he'd be home free.

But he'd knocked No-Neck's across the room and, considering the man currently had his meaty paws around Dylan's throat, there wasn't much hope of getting to it.

Luckily, Eyeballs hadn't fared so well. He'd been the first on the scene, so to speak. When he'd lunged at Dylan as he was closing the door, Dylan had decided to use the door as his best weapon. He'd swung it open as Eyeballs lunged at him. The corner of the door had cracked right against Eyeballs's forehead, and the man had dropped like a deadweight. He was bleeding and moaning now.

But then No-Neck had come out to see what the commotion was. Dylan had considered running, almost sure he could outrun him. But he might lead the guy straight to Vanessa, and he couldn't risk that. Especially if No-Neck had some kind of vehicle.

So he'd fought instead. He'd managed to land a few decent kicks and get the gun away from him, but it had clattered out of reach. Then No-Neck had used his considerable girth to knock Dylan off his feet.

There'd been a moment of panic, which was why Dylan was in his current predicament of having the air slowly choked out of him. If he'd held it together like he had when he'd been a sniper, he would have been able to break the hold.

Still can. Still can. He chanted that to himself even as his vision grayed. He tested the mobility of his legs, feeling the pressure build and build in his head without the ability to take in new air.

One slip of his hand in the right place and he'd—

A gunshot rang out, and No-Neck's body jerked, eyes going wide and then blank as he lurched to the side, lifeless.

Gasping for air, relief coursed through him. Enough that he even closed his eyes. He'd been saved. Saved in the nick of damn time too. His throat ached, his head pounded, but God, he could breathe again and someone...

He opened his eyes, ready to be pissed as hell if Vanessa had come back.

But it wasn't Vanessa.

And he certainly hadn't been saved.

Adele gestured with the gun. "Get up."

Dylan couldn't follow orders because he couldn't make sense of this. "You killed him."

Adele glanced at the lifeless body. "Wasn't as hard as I thought it might be." She glanced at Eyeballs, who was still groaning. Then, before Dylan could even move, she shot him too. Not very cleanly, so she pulled the trigger again. This time, Eyeballs went still.

She turned the gun onto Dylan. She paused there though, not shooting like she had the other two. She watched him, consideration all over her expression.

Dylan didn't let fear enter. He focused on what he could do. She was just a little too far out of reach to knock off her feet, and it would take him a few seconds to regain his clear vision.

"Why are you killing your own men?" he asked incredulously. Surely she wasn't actually saving him.

"My own men are stupid and useless. How many times can they be overpowered by some second-rate unarmed soldier saddled with a pregnant woman?" She cocked her head, still studying him. "You're rather stupid, but you aren't useless yet. Get up."

Slowly, gauging every move she made, every

potential action to grab her weapon, Dylan moved to his feet, but before he could fully straighten from his crouch—which was from where he'd planned to lunge and dislodge the weapon—the gun fired.

The searing stab of pain in his gut had him falling back to his knees. He bit back a howl, his body involuntarily shaking at the unbearable pain in his stomach.

He could feel blood seeping into his shirt, his pants, gushing out of the wound. Gritting his teeth, he sat back on his butt and pushed his hand over the hole. He needed a bandage. Hell, he needed a miracle.

"Sorry. Men with bullets in them are less likely to overpower a poor little woman like me." She shrugged. "Hope I didn't hit one of those internal organs."

Dylan could only hold his hands to the wound, hoping to God she was right. But the blood…

His vision grayed again, so he pressed hard and focused on the pain.

"This would have been easy, Dylan. Simple. But you had to complicate things," Adele said, walking in a circle around him. "No one would be dead if you'd done what you were supposed to. You certainly wouldn't be shot. Don't you always do what you're supposed to?"

"Guess not always," he managed to say between gritted teeth. He needed to get the gun away from her. Preferably before he passed out from blood loss.

"Your perfect daddy knows. About all of it. The sniper nonsense. Vanessa." Adele laughed. "God, I wish I could have seen his face. His precious prince knocking up a Carson. I never *dreamed* I'd get something that good, but you keep *ruining it*."

"Adele. Please, I—"

"Oh, don't patronize me. Don't try to mansplain my life to me."

She waved the gun around, enough to make him nervous. He could maybe survive this bullet wound. He wasn't so sure about another one.

"I'm smarter than you," she said, her knuckles going white on the handle of the gun. "I've always been smarter than you, but somehow you keep ending up on top. Not this time. I'm better. I've always been better."

Dylan fought off a wave of nausea. "If you kill me... Adele, it's over. You don't get any job, any life. *Yours* is over just as much as mine."

"Because you ruined it! I had a plan and you ruined *everything*!" She huffed out a breath and Dylan realized that in this moment in particular she'd lost it. Before, she'd been controlled. She'd had a plan, and he actually believed it hadn't been to kill him.

Now? All bets were off.

"That woman wasn't supposed to be there," she muttered, tapping the gun against the palm of her hand. "You weren't supposed to know how to fight. I rolled with the punches as well as I could, but these two fools were the last straw."

"You can't kill me, Adele."

She raised an eyebrow, and cold, bone-deep fear settled itself in his soul.

He cleared his throat, tried to focus his vision, his brain on anything except the constant wall of pain assaulting him. "Of course you *can* kill me. I'm suggesting it wouldn't be in your best interest."

"And you, of course, would know my best interest. Being a man and all."

He tried to make an argument, but the words sounded jumbled in his head. Everything around him was dim. Had someone turned off a light?

He tightened his grip on his stomach, but he was fading fast.

"I could let you bleed out." She pretended to consider it. "Killing you wasn't in the plans, Dylan. But plans change. Your father told me to be patient. He told me if I proved myself, the job would be mine. And you know what I did? I proved myself. Again and again. Above and beyond, and still *you* got everything."

"What does that have to do with me?"

"You got it. Killing you means you don't have it anymore. And your father suffers. Though I was hoping you'd suffer right along with him when he realized you were a lying, Carson-impregnating disappointment and kicked you out. But death works too."

"You'll miss out on your satisfaction," he managed to slur.

"Maybe. I didn't plan to kill you, Dylan. I just wanted to ruin you." She held the gun up again, this time at his head. "Turns out, I get to do both."

"Like hell." Though he knew it was just as likely to get him killed, he let go of the bullet wound and used his hands to push himself off the ground in the most fluid movement he could manage.

He'd thought to grab the gun, but mostly he just crashed into her. She fell backward, and he fell on top of her. They howled in pain at the same time, the gun clattering to the floor.

Dylan tried to fight, to think, but everything was going black. Pain. So much pain. It was so hard to remember what he was doing or what he was fighting for.

"I'm going to kill her too," Adele screamed, narrowly missing kneeing him in the crotch.

Her. *Them.* Van and his baby. He summoned all his strength, all his focus, shoved the pain away and made a grab for her arms.

His hands were slick with blood from pressing on his wound, and he couldn't manage to hold on to her wrists as she landed blows against his face and then—worse—right where the bullet wound was.

His body went weak and everything became a particular kind of black. Adele made some sound of triumph as she managed to slither away from him.

Dylan couldn't let her win. Couldn't. He struggled to his feet, his balance wavering as Adele rushed over to where the gun had fallen. Using his side that didn't have a bullet wound weakening it, Dylan grabbed the lamp off the table he was standing next to and heaved it at her as hard as he could.

It crashed against her, and she wailed in pain. She began to sway and fall. Or was that him?

A few seconds later, he realized he was on the floor. And someone stood over him.

It wasn't Adele.

It was Grady. And Ty. Carsons. "Am I dead?" Dylan managed to ask. "And in hell?"

Grady swore viciously. "He needs an ambulance. Yesterday." He nodded at Ty, who disappeared from Dylan's wavering vision.

"Adele?"

"If you're talking about the blonde, you knocked her out with that lamp business."

"Where are the police?"

"Setting up they said. They told us to wait. Aren't you lucky we didn't?"

"Grady." He could make out the man's face. Sort of. "Van?"

"Laurel's got her. They're probably on their way up."

"No. Don't let her..." He groaned at the wave of pain, the threat of pure oblivion—or was that death? "Help me up. Get me a clean shirt."

"You need a hospital, moron."

"Yeah. That too. Don't want her to know it's this bad, okay? Just help me... She can't know. Not until a doctor looks at her, okay?"

Dylan didn't really hear Grady's response, but then there were cops running this way and that. Someone ripped off his shirt and pressed a bandage to the wound. He wavered in and out of consciousness, but fought back every time.

He thought he heard Adele screaming, but the most important thing was Vanessa. She needed...

"Come on, tough guy," Grady muttered, pulling a T-shirt over Dylan's head.

"Get me on my feet."

"Ambulance will be here soon. Just sit ti—"

Whatever the cop was saying was cut off by Grady hefting him to his feet. "She's not going to buy this," Grady muttered.

Dylan breathed, letting his body lean against

Grady's. "She'll believe it." One way or another. "I want her checked out and good to go before she knows how bad this is."

Grady shook his head, looping his arm around Dylan's waist. Dylan felt another arm helping him move forward. Ty.

"You're going to be dead before she knows how bad this is," Ty said disgustedly.

"Well, you just make sure she doesn't find that out either until she's talked to a doctor."

"He's got it bad," Grady said.

"Bad? He's got it terminal," Ty replied.

If he lived, yeah, it was damn well going to be terminal.

THE RADIO CALL for an ambulance made Laurel's blood run cold, but she forced herself to smile reassuringly at Vanessa. "They're out." She flicked off the radio, because if they started describing things… Well, as much as she wanted to know what had happened, it was more important to keep Vanessa calm.

She was too pale and even shaking, though Laurel had a sneaking suspicion Vanessa didn't realize her body was reacting to the shock and worry.

"Can we go? I need to see him. I need to be sure…"

"We'll drive up, just as soon as someone gives me an all clear."

"Laurel. If they called an ambulance, doesn't that mean there's an all clear?"

"Not necessarily. Listen—"

She was interrupted by the sound of her phone chiming. She pulled up the text and frowned at Grady's words.

I don't suppose you'd just take Van to a hospital and let us handle all this?

"We're going up," Laurel said. She kept her voice detached and her expression calm, but dread pooled in her stomach.

Surely if Dylan was dead someone would just come out and say it. Surely. She swallowed at the bile that rose in her throat. She'd been a cop long enough to know how to deal with being sick with fear and appear untouched.

She drove too fast up the road toward the cabin Hart had told her about. Two police cruisers, one motorcycle and Grady's truck were parked along the road out of sight, but Laurel drove right up to the cabin.

There were two officers with a handcuffed Adele Oscar. She was bleeding from her head, but clearly yelling at everyone around her. Laurel hoped like hell the cut on her head was the only reason they'd called for an ambulance.

Laurel pulled to a stop. Hart, Grady, Ty and

the other deputy Hart would have taken were nowhere to be seen.

"Stay here and—"

The cabin door opened and, before Laurel
could stop her, Vanessa was out like a shot. Grady
and Ty appeared, Dylan between them.

Vanessa rushed to him, but Laurel held herself
back. There were a few things she noted about
her brother. His face was a mess, but underneath bleeding cuts and blooming bruises, he was
deathly pale. He was wearing what he'd probably
worn to the bank the other morning, except for
the shirt, which she recognized as one of Grady's
T-shirts he often left strewn about the back seat of
his truck. Lastly, Ty was all but holding him up.

But if Vanessa noticed any of those things, it
didn't stop her. She flung her arms around Dylan
and clung tight.

Laurel tried to get ahold of herself as tears
stung her eyes and she felt the weakness in her
muscles. Dylan's eyes weren't focused, even as he
wrapped an arm around Vanessa and murmured
something into her ear.

Slowly, Laurel approached, trying to gauge
anything from Grady's expression, but it was
infuriatingly blank.

"He's hurt. Let's give him some room," Laurel
managed to say gently.

Vanessa sniffled and unwound herself from Dylan. "You need an ambulance."

"Getting one," he said, his mouth curving.

But everything about Dylan was wrong. Faded and weak.

"Van, let me take you down to the hospital. You've got your own knock on the head," Grady said.

He moved away from Dylan, who now leaned even harder on Ty.

"Why can't I just ride in the ambulance with him?" she demanded, pulling her arm out of Grady's grasp.

"You'll have a smoother ride with Grady," Dylan said. His voice was thready.

He was hurt way worse than he was acting, and no one wanted Vanessa to know. Laurel thought about demanding they stop, but Vanessa was a mess herself. Added stress wouldn't help.

"I'm afraid it's procedure," Laurel improvised. "We'll want your statements separately and without the other's perceptions clouding it. We want to make sure Adele goes away for a long time." She touched Vanessa's arm. "You go with Grady and get to the hospital. I'll follow in a minute to get your statement, and Hart will ride with Dylan in the ambulance to get his. Once we've done that, you'll be free to see each other as much as you want."

Vanessa frowned, but Laurel had a sinking suspicion time was of the essence.

"Go on now. We'll get this all sorted ASAP."

Grady managed to lead Vanessa away, though she kept looking back. Dylan managed a smile, but Laurel didn't see anything other than a blankness in it.

"What is it?" Laurel hissed.

"Just wait," Dylan muttered.

His gaze stayed on Vanessa's retreating form until it disappeared around the corner, then his whole face went slack. He swore weakly.

"What *is* it?"

Since Dylan looked like he was in the middle of passing out, she turned her glare to Ty.

"He was shot. In the gut. That ambulance of yours better be quick."

"Get him on the ground," Laurel barked. "What the hell is wrong with you? Letting him stand up? Are you stupid?" Her voice cracked on the last word, and she helped Ty lower Dylan to the ground.

Laurel kneeled next to him, berating him the whole way. "How can you be this stupid?"

"Don't cry, sis."

"I'm not crying," she retorted, even though the tears were rolling big and fat down her face. "What are you doing getting yourself shot? That's my job," she managed, hoping to keep him talking, keep him awake. As long as he was awake…

"I'll be okay. Probably. Tradition, right? You, then Cam. Now me. Someone better get Jen a bulletproof vest."

"Not funny. Stay with me, okay? Stay with me." She took his hand and squeezed it. "You've got an awful lot of explaining to do, so you can't go."

He didn't squeeze back and his eyes were closed, but he kept talking. "Damnedest thing, Laurel. I love her. I don't know how it happened. It was like…there. Just there."

"Yeah, I get that." *Keep him talking. Keep him talking.* "One minute you think they're the bane of your existence and then you realize they were just…meant to be part of your existence."

"Meant to be. I never believed in meant to be, but I believed in a feud. How backward is that?"

"Nothing's backward if you right the ship." She could hear the faint sound of sirens and prayed they'd hurry. She pressed Dylan's palm to her cheek. It was bloody and beat up, and she couldn't hold back the sob that escaped her mouth.

"Laurel. Don't worry so much. It's going to take more than a bullet to stop me from being a father. Better one than ours."

It shocked her to hear Dylan say that. He'd

been Dad's staunchest supporter, and he certainly didn't know about Dad's outburst earlier.

"Better than ours," Laurel agreed. "And you'll have to work on your uncle skills too, okay?"

"Uncle. You too?" He chuckled, though it sounded more like a wet wheeze that had Laurel crying all over again. "That's a trip. That's a—"

"All right." Laurel looked up, relief almost making her pass out as the ambulance came into view. "Time to show us how strong you are."

"I'll be okay. I'll be okay. Tell Van I'll be okay, yeah?"

Laurel got out of the way of the paramedics and turned away from watching them work. When she felt a hand squeeze her shoulder, she turned to see it was Ty.

"Come on. Let's get to the hospital."

She nodded, pulling herself together bit by bit. There was still a lot of work to do.

Chapter Nineteen

"Definitely a nasty bump, and the short-term amnesia is concerning, but it's probably more a response to trauma than head injury. Though you'll want to pay specific attention to headaches, vision problems, anything that might point to an underlying issue."

Vanessa nodded at the doctor and bit her tongue so she didn't say something like, *"I don't give a damn about me. Tell me about the baby."*

"Baby's heartbeat is strong. I don't think you'll have anything to worry about there, though I'd make a follow-up appointment with your ob just to be sure they don't have any concerns."

"So the baby's okay?"

"Seems to be."

Vanessa slid off the exam table. "So I can go?"

"Your blood pressure is high. I'd like to keep you here and see if it levels. So let's have a seat and relax."

Vanessa glared at Grady. "Did he just tell me to relax?"

"Come on, Van." Grady nodded the doctor to the door, and the doctor did the first intelligent thing since he'd opened it—he left without a word.

Grady ushered her back to the exam bed. "Listen to the doctor," he said gently, urging her back onto the bed.

She went, but she folded her arms across her chest and glared. "I want to see Dylan."

"He's getting checked out, same as you."

Now that she had time to think, there'd been something very wrong in that whole scene outside the cabin. Dylan hadn't been himself. But he'd been standing there, talking to her.

She *hated* this feeling that she was missing a piece. Laurel had questioned her earlier, looking pale and distracted, and informed her Adele was being treated for her injuries and then would be released into police custody.

But she couldn't tell her Dylan's condition or what he'd said in his statement or what would happen to that awful woman.

"Where's Laurel?"

"She told you. She went to check on Dylan."

"*I* want to check on Dylan."

Grady gave her his patented raised-eyebrow look. "Funny thing, that."

Vanessa looked away. She wasn't embarrassed. Not after everything she and Dylan had been through, but there was a certain discomfort over the fact she'd given Grady such a hard time about getting together with Laurel and now she… "How did it happen?"

"How did what happen?" Grady asked, scooting the too-small chair he was balanced on closer to her bed.

"Us. How did we… How are they…?" She shook her head, feeling overwhelmed and emotional. "I love him. I don't know how. I don't know what did it, but I love him. So much it's scary. A *Delaney.*"

"Yeah, kinda hits you over the head like that." He took her hand in his and gave it a squeeze. "I couldn't tell you why. I can only tell you if it feels right, it is."

Vanessa nodded, blinking back unruly tears. "I need him to be okay."

"Then he'll be okay."

"Because I have such a great track record of getting what I need?"

"Because he's a Delaney, and they do." He touched her hair gently. "You gave us quite the scare."

"You should have known I'd kick my way out of it." All those emotions inside her wanted to lean into her big brother and just sob them away, but she felt trapped. Until she knew for sure Dylan was okay…

"Something's wrong."

"It only feels that way because you've been through this crazy thing. Time's only going slow because you're waiting. But you aren't getting out of here until that blood pressure comes down, so why don't you try to rest?"

Because she wouldn't be able to. She couldn't *rest* until she was out of this claustrophobic room and she could hold Dylan again.

Something wasn't right. Something hadn't been right for a while, but she wasn't going to get answers until that doctor let her out of here, so she closed her eyes and breathed.

She was more than grateful Grady didn't drop her hand. He held it the whole time, and it became an anchor.

Time passed interminably, but no matter how many times she asked, Grady didn't have any information. When the doctor returned what felt like a million years later, her blood pressure had gone down enough that he felt comfortable releasing her.

Which took another million years, with paperwork and instructions, warnings of headaches and blah, blah, blah. Her baby was fine and she needed to know why the hell she hadn't seen Dylan yet.

"I just need to use the bathroom. You want to wait here?" she asked, pointing at some chairs in the lobby.

Luckily, Grady was distracted enough by texting with Ty that he didn't look at her to see the lie.

"Sure." He took a seat and kept typing on his phone.

Vanessa walked casually toward the restrooms but then kept going. She found a map, tried to decide where Dylan would be. He'd come in an ambulance, so Emergency probably. She started backtracking to where she'd been treated in Emergency, but before she made it there she saw a cop going in the opposite direction. She knew him. Something Hart. He worked with Laurel a lot.

He didn't see her, and she made sure he didn't. She turned, waited, then casually started tailing him at a reasonable pace.

At one point he looked back, but there was a large gentleman in front of her who blocked his view.

When he pushed open the doors for the surgery wing, Vanessa's heart dropped and she didn't bother to keep her pace slow or calm herself. She ran forward, then came to a stumbling stop at the row of chairs occupied by Delaneys.

"Oh, my God."

Laurel jumped to her feet, swearing under her breath as she came up to Vanessa. "Don't jump to the worst conclusion."

"You're all here."

Jen's face was blotchy, and so was Laurel's. Hilly, Vanessa's long-lost cousin and Cam's girlfriend, was dabbing her eyes with a Kleenex.

"You're all crying," Vanessa accused, pointing wildly. *God, no. No.*

"Not all of us. Cam isn't crying," Laurel offered hopefully. When Vanessa only looked at her in horror, Laurel hooked arms with her and continued. "Look, Dylan's in surgery."

"For *what*?" Vanessa demanded, wrestling her arm away from Laurel's grasp.

Grady stormed through the doors, face etched in furious lines. "Damn it, Van. You told me you were going to the bathroom."

"And you told me everything was fine!" She whirled back to Laurel. "Why is he in surgery?"

"He was…shot."

"Shot? *Shot?* When? How could he have been…?" She swayed on her feet but Grady grabbed her and pushed her into a seat next to Hilly. It dawned on Vanessa why everything had been wrong since that moment. "He was shot before we got there. He was *hiding* it from me."

"Yes," Laurel agreed.

"Why?" She looked up helplessly at Laurel,

then Grady. She'd give Dylan a piece of her mind once he was out of surgery. Oh, boy, would she. "How long? What are they— Tell me what you know."

"Let's just—"

"Tell me what you know." She grabbed Laurel's arms, trying to get it through the woman's thick skull. "I don't care what he wanted kept from me. I don't care about anything except knowing what's going on. I *need* to know what he's going through."

Laurel softened, but her eyes filled again. She ruthlessly blinked those tears away, putting on that cop face Vanessa had to admit she envied.

"He was shot in the stomach," Laurel said, and she might have sounded like some detached cop if her voice wasn't so scratchy. "Unfortunately, it did hit some organs, which means he could be in surgery for a while. Right now, all we can do is wait for the surgeon to do his job and then let us know how it went."

"He might die." It slammed through her, the understanding. Why he'd been trying to shield her from knowing. He might legitimately *die*.

"Van, listen—"

She looked up at Laurel, fury and fear causing her to shake. "He might *die*. Don't *'listen'* me. It's true. He might die."

"It's true," she said, though her voice was an unsteady whisper.

"But he might not," Hilly said, taking Vanessa's hand in hers. Her voice was calm and collected. Soothing. Not detached like Laurel's. "No use focusing on the worst-case scenario when it's not the only option. Focus on—on—"

"Healing thoughts," Jen supplied. "Prayers, vibes, whatever you got."

Vibes. Prayers. Thoughts. Vanessa wanted to scream. None of it mattered. None of it helped. "It's a curse. It's true. I didn't believe in curses, but here we are."

Grady crouched in front of her. Her brother who'd happily talked about feuds and being better than Delaneys for most of his life. He took her hands in his, looked right at her, certain and sure.

"There is no curse. Love is never a curse. New life is no curse. This is a challenge, but not a curse. And if we beat all these challenges, can you imagine what we'll have?"

No feud? Carsons and Delaneys all intermingled? Not so long ago she would have told anyone who listened that that was her worst nightmare.

But somehow it had become her brightest dream, so she did what Jen said. She prayed. She thought about healing. She sent all the energy she could muster into the universe.

And in a waiting room full of Carsons and Delaneys holding hands and murmuring encouragement to each other, Vanessa waited.

THE DESERT WAS never ending. And why was he wearing all these clothes? A cowboy hat, of all damn things? He was riding a horse through the desert and all he wanted was a drink of water.

His body hurt everywhere, rivers of fiery pain. He looked down. Bullet holes, but no blood.

He tried to make the image go away, since it couldn't possibly be real, but the scene just kept playing out. He could see it, like a movie, and yet it was him. He could feel the cowboy hat. The weird scratchy pants and boots that fit like a second skin.

But he was full of bullet holes.

When he looked up, there was another horse. Another rider. He was in white. She was in black.

She.

"Vanessa?"

The black flowed around her as she rode toward him—the fabric of her clothes, the long strands of her hair. The wind whipped her skirts and scarves and she had a hat. A bright, shiny skull glinted on her hat. It looked just about perfect.

Her horse pounded through the sand, closer and closer and yet not close enough.

A choice. Somehow he knew that somewhere,

there was a choice. Take the bullet holes and go to her. Doomed.

Turn away and everything would be fine. He could turn his horse in the opposite direction and the bullet holes would heal and all would be well.

Except she wouldn't be his. He was alive, maybe? Bullet holes and all, but no blood. Pain, yes, but you had to be alive to feel pain.

Why would he turn away?

He fell off the horse into the sand, but it didn't feel like sand. It felt like a bed.

He blinked his eyes open and...the desert was gone. He still needed a drink of water, desperately. But everything was dim instead of blinding. All he could think was she was gone. The horse and her swirling black costume.

"Van."

"There you are."

Her voice. God, he thought he might cry. But he didn't. He couldn't seem to move his head toward her voice. "You were all dressed up," he muttered, realizing somewhat belatedly it had been a dream. Just a silly, weird-as-hell dream.

"Can't even have a sex dream right?"

"I can't...move."

"That's okay." He felt her hand on one shoulder, then she moved into his line of sight. "They said you'll be out of sorts and they've got you hooked up to all sorts of things. Just lie still."

He drank her in. She looked good. Healthy and sturdy. Not pale. She wasn't swathed in black layers, but instead wore jeans and a T-shirt. Still, she looked so good and so *his*, he didn't think it could be real. "Am I dead?"

"Not unless the dead can speak. And all those doctors and nurses prodding at you day and night seem to think you'll recover. I guess you don't remember waking up? You've been in and out."

"I don't remember much of anything since Adele shot me. Except that I felt dead there for a while."

"Yes, well, speaking of that. You're lucky you're laid up because I'd like to kick your butt to Toledo." She slid onto the edge of his bed, studying his face intently. Her dark eyes were hard to read, but he thought he saw relief.

"I don't have much interest in going to Ohio, so I guess that works, all in all." He closed his eyes, feeling unbearably exhausted. "Are you going to touch me or what?"

She made a sound that was almost a laugh, and then he felt her shift next to him, stretching out in the small amount of bed space available. "They're going to come in and yell at me, but I don't care."

"Good, I don't either."

"Dylan Delaney, you always care about the rules and what's right."

"Nah, that's just what people think." He nuzzled into her. "I want to hold you."

"Well, you'll have to settle for me holding you for now." Her arms came around him and he sighed into her. Because one arm was close to her, he managed to inch it toward her belly. He touched her stomach, fitting his hand over the softest swell.

"Baby's fine," she murmured, her fingers feeling like heaven against his hair.

"What about mama?"

"Mama." He felt her whoosh of breath against his face. It felt like heaven. "You know, it's funny, I hadn't really thought in terms of *mama* yet."

"Well, you've got some time to get used to that. And the fact you're going to have to marry me."

She was quiet for a while. He worked up the energy to open his eyes. She was looking at the IV hooked up to him, and all the other machines that seemed to keep beeping at him unnecessarily.

She met his gaze. "Never really figured I'd get married. I'm not much of a traditionalist."

"I am. But I can be flexible. We'll hyphenate our names."

Vanessa snorted. "You want our child to walk around Bent, Wyoming, with the names Delaney and Carson together?"

"I do," he returned. "You can keep your name. I'll keep mine. Baby will have both. You'll keep your shop. I—I don't know what my position is at the bank, but I can get a job at Cam's security business if I have to."

"Mr. Secret Sniper."

"I was thinking more along the lines of accounting. I think my sniper days are behind me." He gestured helplessly. "I don't know if you noticed, but I got beat to hell back there."

She closed her eyes, an expression of pain taking over her face. "Yeah, I noticed." She held him a little tighter, though he could tell she was being exceptionally gentle. He wished he didn't feel like he needed it.

"So, your plan is…you're going to marry me?"

"Damn straight."

"In front of your father and the rest of your family, in front of Bent citizens, you're going to promise to love and cherish a Carson?"

Though it felt like flaming hot needles in his side and shoulder, he lifted her hand to his mouth and pressed a kiss to her palm. "Till death do us part."

"Are you sure you don't have a head injury?"

"I might have several for all I know." He sighed, letting his arm fall back down, his eyes drifting closed. "But I'm sure I'm going to marry you. If you want to wait to decide until we make sure my body's in working order again, that's fine. But I can tell you right here, right now, I love you. And we're going to get married. Bullet holes or no."

"Holes? Pretty sure you were only shot once."

"I dreamed there were bullet holes all over the place. But I had a choice. Live through them with you, or walk away. I didn't walk then. I'm not going to, ever."

"You aren't making any sense."

He muttered something and slid back into dreams. There weren't bullet holes this time. No horses or desert. Just a quiet porch.

He awoke a few times, mostly to nurses poking and prodding him. Once Laurel was there with Grady. Twice it was Jen. A few times it was Cam and Hilly. And always, every single time, Vanessa was there too.

The next day when he woke it was dark, and it wasn't to a nurse poking at him. He just surfaced naturally. Vanessa was curled against him, fast asleep.

Unable to resist, he brushed some hair off her face. She hadn't left him. Maybe a hospital wasn't the real world yet, but it was real enough. This wasn't going to evaporate. They were going to make it work.

She stirred, blinked open her eyes and yawned. "You're still too weak for sex, buddy."

He didn't laugh because he knew it would hurt

his side, but he smiled. "Noted. They let you stay in here?"

"Tried to kick me out. Even threatened to call security. I just snuck back in."

"Mmm, have I mentioned I love you?"

She snuggled closer. "Not enough."

He managed to move more than he had yet. He turned his head and kissed her temple. "Decided to marry me yet?"

She shook her head. "You're relentless. I thought the bullet hole and massive blood loss might slow you down."

"Your family and mine both donated blood. I'm just filled to the brim with relentless now."

She laughed at that, and he couldn't get over being able to lie with her, make her laugh. The pain didn't matter. The circumstances. She was his. And they'd made it through.

"You going to move in to my shop?"

"No."

"You think I'm going to move onto the Delaney ranch?"

This time he laughed, then winced at the wave of pain. "No. Not in a million years." He frowned, realizing something he hadn't quite put together till she'd mentioned the ranch. "My father. Everyone has been in here except..."

Vanessa stiffened, then slowly exhaled. "Well, you know he has a lot to clean up at the bank."

Dylan maneuvered so he could look down incredulously at her, but it hurt so he ended up just kind of flopping around. "Are you defending my father?"

"No. I think he's a dirty rotten bastard." Vanessa blew out a breath, rubbing her hand over his shoulder. "Let's not talk about your dad."

"He really hasn't been by, has he? He…" Dylan couldn't wrap his head around it. He'd almost died.

Well, he supposed it told him all he needed to know. No matter how much it hurt, his father wasn't the man Dylan had thought him to be. Dylan closed his eyes. His body hurt. His head hurt. His *heart* hurt.

"So where are we going to live if I marry you?" Vanessa prodded. "My answer depends on that."

She was trying to distract him. Why not let her? "Well, I'd consider your shop except I'm pretty sure there's no way on earth to baby proof it. We need some room. A house to build our family in." He thought about the cabin they'd been stuck in, then chuckled a little to himself at the fact it'd likely be on the market eventually. "I know a cabin that's going to be up for sale."

She laughed. "Yeah, let's buy Adele's cabin and live there. How much of your blood are we going to have to scrub out of the floorboards?"

"It *is* where we fell in love," he said, warming

to the idea. "Isolated and away from Bent. Even if we didn't live there full-time, it could be our vacation home. I'd miss ranch life, but being outside of town would be good enough."

"It's only a twenty-minute drive to town. We'd both be able to get to work." She gently slapped his chest. "No. What am I saying?" She laughed again, and it was like heaven to hear her laugh. Soothed all the rough edges, the pain and the disappointment.

Maybe he didn't have his father anymore, but he had something bigger. Greater. A family who cared. *Family.* Love. No more feud nonsense or pointless bitterness. He was going to embrace the good.

"We're not buying Adele's cabin," Vanessa said firmly.

"I don't know. Something to think about."

"You go back to sleep. Wake up with an ounce of sense in your head."

He kissed her temple again, since he could, and then decided he would go back to sleep. But he wouldn't make any promises about sense.

Chapter Twenty

Vanessa was exhausted. Sleeping in a hospital wasn't exactly restful, fighting with nurses and doctors even less so. But Dylan was getting released tomorrow and…

He'd have to go back to the Delaney Ranch for a while. She couldn't take care of him in her shop, much as she wanted to.

She'd made a promise to herself back in her teenage years that she'd never, ever step foot on the Delaney Ranch again, but she was going to have to break that promise to herself. For Dylan. For their future.

Which meant she had to clear some air. She'd left Dylan after his meeting with the doctor to discuss rehabilitation. Jen had planned on spending the day with him while Vanessa did what she had to do.

First up? Something long overdue.

She knocked on the door to Laurel and Grady's

house, knowing Grady would be at Rightful Claim getting ready for opening.

Laurel opened the door looking bleary-eyed and miserable.

"Oh, so I see it's hit you too."

Laurel groaned. "I felt fine. Maybe a little tired. Dizzy sometimes. Then this morning? Barf city."

"I'd love to tell you it gets better."

Laurel groaned again, motioning Vanessa inside.

Weirdly, the shared morning sickness both put her at ease and somehow made this harder. "So, um."

Laurel waited patiently, but all Vanessa could do was stutter. Irritated with herself, she decided some things didn't need to change. Including her *go-for-it* attitude.

"We used to be best friends," she blurted.

Laurel blinked, then nodded slowly. "Yeah, we were."

"I haven't really had one since. A best friend."

Laurel's confused expression softened. "Me neither. I mean, there's your brother, but his eyes glaze over when I want to discuss the romantic overtures in a movie."

Vanessa managed a weak laugh. "Hey, my eyes used to glaze over too."

"No, you pretended, but you watched all those rom-coms right along with me."

Years ago. Something like a lifetime. How was Vanessa expecting to go back to that? Of course, how was she expecting to marry Dylan Delaney? Life just didn't make sense. "I guess I was hoping we could be friends again."

Laurel grinned. "Van. We aren't friends."

Vanessa frowned. Why was she grinning at that? Laurel wasn't *mean*. But that was a mean thing to say. "Well, screw y—"

Laurel rolled her eyes and stepped forward. "We're *sisters*." She held out her hands like it was as simple as that.

For Laurel, it was. And Vanessa was beginning to realize, after coming through the hardest, scariest, most complicated moment in her life, that sometimes simple was the best way to go.

"Do you really believe all that stuff Grady said in the waiting room about no curses, just challenges? Do you really believe that?"

"I do. I'll admit when you and Dylan were both missing, I wondered. I doubted. But…" She shook her head, then placed both hands over her stomach. "How could I ever think this was wrong? Cursed?"

Vanessa put her hands over her own stomach. It wasn't a curse. The baby had never, ever felt like one, even when she'd been certain she'd write Dylan out of their lives forever. "Us both pregnant at the same time? Kinda feels more like fate than a curse."

This time, Laurel gave her a hug. "Fate," she said, squeezing tight. "I like that a lot."

Vanessa squeezed her back, uncomfortable with all this baring of her soul and whatnot, but she wasn't quite done. "Listen." She pulled away. "There's something else I wanted to talk to you about. Your dad hasn't been by to visit Dylan."

Laurel blew out a breath then made her way over to the couch and sank into it. She gestured for Vanessa to do the same. "No, he hasn't."

"Dylan wants to go see him when he's released tomorrow. I don't want him to go if your dad's going to be a jerk."

"Then you'll have to stop him, because the bottom line is my dad's going to be a jerk."

"I don't get it. I mean, I always hated your dad but he didn't whale on you. I figured…you know, that meant he was a good dad at least, even if he was a snobby jerk."

"I don't get it either. That's not the man I knew. Sure, the feud was important to him, but his family was the *most* important thing. But…"

"He came to your wedding."

"Yeah. I thought that meant something. Turns out he thought I'd come to my senses before I started popping out babies."

"That's awful."

"It's sad. He's sad." Laurel reached over and took Vanessa's hand. "I know you want to protect Dylan. I do too. But he's going to need to face him. Talk to him. If it ends badly, you'll be there to support him. Trust me. It won't make it not hurt, but it helps."

"You know, I think you're good for Grady."

Laurel raised her eyes. "Are you sneaking Dylan's painkillers?"

Vanessa rolled her eyes. "He needed someone to depend on but not another Carson dude. You. You're... I've been awful and I think it's because I knew..." Vanessa pulled a face. "I'm about to be barf city too."

"Yeah, because you're talking about your feelings, not because you're having morning sickness."

"I guess you've still got my number."

"Well enough, anyway."

"It's just... I knew you were better for him. I resented that. I resented you and him both getting over all that crap they've been feeding us since we were babies. The feud was safe. No one got hurt with it."

"And no one got any better either."

"Yeah, I'm figuring that out. I don't want your father to hurt him."

"I know. He probably will. You won't be able to shield Dylan from that hurt any more than he'll be able to, say, give birth to that baby for you, though I know he'd take all that pain on himself if he could. Love, I've discovered, doesn't really solve all our problems."

"So what *does* it do?"

"Gives us a hand to hold to get through the problems with. Which actually works out a lot better than just avoiding pain."

"If you say so," Vanessa muttered. But much as it sounded like a load of crock, Vanessa had no reason not to trust Laurel. And that felt pretty damn good.

DYLAN MIGHT HAVE kissed the ground if he wasn't in a world of pain. Still, he was free. Free. Walking of his own accord out of the hospital, not to return.

Except for rehabilitation and checkups and blah, blah, blah. But he'd focus on his freedom.

And what he had to do. The sun was shining and the sky was a vibrant blue. It felt like a fresh new start.

It would be, once he dealt with this one cloud over his head. First, he had to get rid of Vanessa and preferably one sister. In an ideal world, he'd get rid of all of them, but he wasn't cleared to drive just yet.

"I've never had so many females fluttering

over me in my life. Remind me never to get shot again."

"Remind yourself, hotshot. I wasn't the one playing Mr. Hero and shoving me out the door, then pretending like you hadn't been shot. You'd probably be in better shape if you'd owned up to it."

"The ambulance would have gotten there at the same time either way. Besides, your blood pressure was high enough."

Vanessa crossed her arms over her chest as they stopped outside the hospital doors. "I can't believe Grady blabbed to you about that. Besides, I was *fine*."

"We'll go get the car. You two sit tight." Laurel smiled and pulled Jen away.

"They're giving us privacy to argue."

Dylan tilted his face up to the sun. "Yeah. Or themselves privacy to gossip."

"I want to go with you," Vanessa said firmly.

He didn't need a translator to figure out her abrupt subject change. "It's just not a great idea."

"I'm not afraid of your father."

"I'm not afraid of him either. That's why I'm going to talk to him, but you being there is only going to irritate him."

She glared. "Good. A man can't visit his on-death's-door son in the hospital, he can stand to be a little irritated."

Dylan tried to hold on to the contentment he felt over being out of the hospital, but tension was creeping into his shoulders. "It'll be better for all of us—"

"No. We're done with that. I'll let you handle the crazy lunatics with guns since you know how to handle yourself, but you're not deciding what's right for us. That's not how this goes."

"You're exhausting."

"Get used to it."

"You have to know some of the things he's going to say, and I don't really want an audience for how awful he can be. I don't want you to feel—"

"What? You're not really afraid I'll have second thoughts?"

Laurel pulled the car to the curb and Dylan started to move for it, but Vanessa stopped him.

"Babe, I ain't ever cared what this town or your father thought, and I'm not about to start now. In fact, I think I'm going to take out an ad in the paper and make a big old banner that says 'PREGNANT WITH DYLAN DELANEY'S BABY AND PROUD OF IT.' I'll hang it above Rightful Claim so everyone can see."

He took her hand, brought it to his mouth and brushed a kiss across her knuckles. "I love you."

"And I love you. Which means I'm not leaving

your side no matter how many Delilah references your father makes."

Dylan looked at her. Really looked at her. He'd accepted he'd fallen in love with her despite previous incidents. She was strong and brave and awe-inspiring. He wanted to build a life with her because she fit, perfectly, like she'd always belonged at his side.

But he'd never fully grasped the simple fact that Vanessa Carson would be *good* for him. He'd spent far too long caring what people thought— not enough to capitulate always, but enough to lie or cover it up when he didn't.

Vanessa wouldn't do that, and he didn't think she'd let him do it either. He knew she wouldn't let their kid grow up feeling like they had to be something they weren't.

"Why are you looking at me like that? Your sisters are waiting."

"You're right."

Her eyebrows rose. "Well, I know I am. So, you're not going to fight me coming with you?"

He linked his fingers with hers and moved to the car. "No. No, you're right. We're a team. No more lone-wolf stuff."

They climbed in the back seat of Jen's car and chatted casually on the way over to the Delaney

Ranch, but the tension that crept into the car the closer they got didn't escape Dylan's notice.

"Can you guys let me and Van do this on our own?"

Jen nodded. "Of course. We'll go down to Hilly's, and you just holler if you need anything."

"Appreciate it."

Much as it grated, he had to let Vanessa help him out of the car. Even though it had been a mostly smooth ride, he felt jostled and achy. This whole recovery thing was not going to be a walk in the park.

But walking up to the door with Vanessa's hand in his was a soothing balm to that pain, and he had to believe that would always be the case.

He opened the door and led her inside. He called out for his father once, but it was soon clear he wasn't on the main floor. Must be upstairs in his office.

Dylan was exhausted. He lowered himself onto the living-room couch. "Need a minute before we head upstairs," he muttered.

"I'll go get him," Vanessa said, already striding toward the stairs.

"Van."

She gave him an arch look.

"Teamwork, remember?" He patted the spot on the couch next to him.

She wrinkled her nose then huffed out a breath before she plopped herself next to him on the couch.

"Man, you got some fancy digs, Delaney."

"It's no above-business apartment, but it'll do in a pinch."

She smiled at him, then brushed her fingers over his hair. "You're wiped."

"Yeah. I'll live though."

"I'll make sure of it." She kissed his cheek. Her random acts of gentleness never failed to move him.

"I love you, Van."

"I love you too."

Footsteps sounded on the stairs that led into the living room. "Gird your loins," Dylan muttered.

Dad appeared at the base of the stairs. There was a moment of shock in his expression, then something more like pain. He cleared his throat. He looked...rough, Dylan decided. There was no wave of sympathy though, because he'd been in the hospital for *days*, and not once had Dad been by.

Didn't that tell him everything?

He'd had a plan to ask his dad how things were. To be calm and kind when he asked where they stood. But that plan evaporated.

"I'm only here to get my things," Dylan announced. A man who'd made the mistakes his father had and still refused to see his son in the hospital wasn't worth an attempt at civility.

"Dylan."

"No. No, I can't stay here. Not under this roof. I thought I could be reasonable, but I just keep thinking of Adele telling me she'd been promised my job and—"

"She was a good employee, but she needed motivation. My handling of the situation hardly made her kidnap you and—"

"Shoot me? Try to kill me? Maybe it didn't *make* her do that, but it certainly didn't help. Your manipulations and lies…all the hurt they caused." He pushed himself into a standing position. "I won't be a part of it. *We* won't be a part of it. I'll get my things and we'll find somewhere else to—"

"Perhaps we can come to an agreement where you both stay here," Dad interrupted, his businessman-negotiation tone of voice firmly in place.

Dylan sank right back onto the couch, all his energy whooshing out of him with that bombshell. "Excuse me?"

"You certainly don't *have* to, but the offer is open if it might help your rehabilitation. I'm sure you could make room for Vanessa in your room. She'd be welcome."

"Okay, we'll take you up on that."

Dylan looked incredulously at the woman

who'd once said something like she'd rather drink bleach than live at the Delaney ranch. "We will?"

"Temporarily. Until you're recovered enough to do it all on your own." Vanessa looked imperiously at his father. "Thank you."

"It's settled, then."

Vanessa nodded firmly. "Settled."

Dylan pushed his fingers to his temple. "I think I'm hallucinating."

"No. Your sister said some things to me that…" Dad blew out a breath. He was clearly flummoxed and irritated, but instead of retreating or putting on his usual cool disdain, Dad ran a hand through his hair. "I've made mistakes. I don't regret all of them. But I've been…wrong a time or two. It isn't comfortable or joyful for me that you've all decided to…"

Dad shook his head, trailing off and then pacing. He stopped, looking at Dylan and Vanessa. He drew into that ramrod posture that Dylan was used to seeing precede a lecture. "I've been working with some lawyers about setting up trusts."

"Trusts?"

"For your child, and Laurel's. That's simple fact, and regardless of circumstances they will be my grandchildren. My grandchildren will have the best."

"Your grandchildren will have a choice," Vanessa replied.

Dad clearly wanted to say something to that. But he didn't.

Dylan was pretty sure he was hallucinating. Maybe Vanessa had slipped him one of those painkillers that made him loopy.

"Family is the most important thing. Which isn't the same as our name, I suppose."

The *"I suppose"* almost made Dylan smile. But he wouldn't put Vanessa through his father's behavior. "There will be rules."

"Of course. As long as Vanessa is the mother of your child, I'll treat her with the amount of respect that entails."

"Now I think *I'm* hallucinating," Vanessa muttered.

"I've made some mistakes and things have gotten out of hand these past few years. Everything, really. Well, that won't do. We're still Delaneys. So instead of falling apart, we'll—" Dad made a face, but Dylan gave him some credit for continuing "—work together. Make adjustments and a few compromises. Maybe…maybe Laurel was right and that's been the answer for this town all along."

Vanessa's hand curled around Dylan's and squeezed. "I think working together is just what we need."

Dylan squeezed her hand back. He'd spent most of his life hating Carsons and everything they

stood for. He'd never imagined himself here…
being part of a linking of the Delaney and Carson names.

But he'd never been prouder of anything in his life.

Epilogue

Two months later

"You guys know this is the most insane thing possible?"

Vanessa swung on the porch swing Dylan had installed yesterday, while their families helped move furniture and boxes so neither Vanessa nor Dylan would overexert themselves in their move from the Delaney Ranch to their new place.

"Are you talking about *us* or the cabin?"

Laurel eased onto the spot next to Vanessa. They'd both gotten much bigger recently. Once Vanessa and Dylan were all moved in, they were going to have a joint baby shower. Then in no time at all, their babies would be born just two months apart.

It felt like it was taking forever.

"I suppose you heard about Adele's insanity plea," Laurel said softly.

Vanessa shrugged. She'd had to let some things

go in her life. Anger toward Adele was one of them. She'd never forgive that woman for the hell she'd put them through, but she wouldn't waste her energy being angry over it. "Long as she's locked up, I don't care if it's a jail or an asylum."

Laurel looked at the cabin again and shook her head. "I can't believe you want to live in the house you were basically held prisoner in."

Van smiled at the gleaming wood, her brother and cousins hefting in couches and bed frames while Dylan's brothers surreptitiously handed him only the lightest of boxes.

"I fell in love with your brother here. Why wouldn't we want to raise our family here?"

Laurel only shook her head again. "If you say so."

Dylan crossed the porch, eased himself next to Vanessa. "I think that's it."

Vanessa studied his face. She'd been worried he'd overexert himself. He was mostly back to normal, but still working on endurance and range of motion, and he tended to push himself.

But she didn't see signs of extra fatigue or that awful gray note to his complexion he sometimes got. He'd held up well, and it allowed her to relax.

"Cam and Hilly are going to get the pizza. They treated me like a damn toddler when I suggested I could get it myself."

Van patted his shoulder. "You get toddler status a little while longer."

Dylan rested his hand on the rounded mound of her belly, and they both sighed contentedly. Home. They were home. And about to be a family. Whatever hell they'd been through, it had been worth this moment right here. Them. Their families. A future.

Vanessa nodded at Ty, who was standing by the moving van looking standoffish and moody. Then Jen, who was all but hiding behind Grady as she chatted with her cousin, Gracie. "Have you guys noticed those two act like they have a magnet repelling them at all times?"

"No," Dylan replied, frowning.

"Oh, totally," Laurel said. "I'm almost *certain* they had a thing in high school."

"Jen and Ty?" Dylan demanded incredulously. "No way."

"Way. Then he went off into the army. I don't think I've seen them exchange more than two words in the year he's been back."

"Maybe they just don't like each other." Dylan patted Vanessa's belly. "Not everyone falls in love with the enemy," he said with a wink.

Vanessa shook her head. "There's something there, and at some point? It's going to explode. Happened to us. Don't know why it wouldn't happen to them."

Dylan studied his sister, and then Vanessa's cousin. He shook his head. "No way."

Laurel got up off the swing as Grady sauntered over. "Mark me down in the *something-is-there* column," she offered, walking to meet her husband.

Vanessa looked at *her* husband—a term she surprisingly loved, as much as she had their simple courthouse wedding and raucous after-party at the Carson ranch—and grinned. "How much you want to bet those two hook up by the end of the year?" she said, nodding back toward Jen.

Dylan rubbed his hand over his chin, studying Ty, then Jen again. He named the same astronomical sum he'd named at Laurel and Grady's wedding. The night that had changed both their lives for the absolute best.

She leaned over and kissed the scar on his eyebrow, a parting gift from No-Neck, he liked to say. "Delaneys always love to flaunt their money," she murmured.

He linked his hand with hers. "These days, I hear tell, Delaney-Carsons love to flaunt their love."

She rolled her eyes, but she leaned into him, content to swing on the porch swing with her husband, watching their family—all those intertwined Carsons and Delaneys—interact and love and laugh.

Yeah, that was definitely something to flaunt, enjoy and nurture.

Forever.

* * * * *

Don't miss the next book in
Nicole Helm's
Carson & Delaneys: Battle Tested miniseries:

Wyoming Cowboy Ranger

Available June 2019 wherever
Harlequin Intrigue books and ebooks are sold.

Get 4 FREE REWARDS!

We'll send you 2 FREE Books plus 2 FREE Mystery Gifts.

RANCHER'S HIGH-STAKES RESCUE
Beth Cornelison

KILLER SMILE
Marilyn Pappano

Harlequin® Romantic Suspense books feature heart-racing sensuality and the promise of a sweeping romance set against the backdrop of suspense.

FREE Value Over $20

Get 4 FREE REWARDS!

We'll send you 2 FREE Books plus 2 FREE Mystery Gifts.

Harlequin Presents® books feature a sensational and sophisticated world of international romance where sinfully tempting heroes ignite passion.

FREE Value Over **$20**